M.I. Scarrott

Out of the
Miry Clay

— A N O V E L —

M. I. Scarrott

Out of the
Miry Clay

— A N O V E L —

*"He brought me up also out of an horrible pit, out of the miry clay,
And set my feet upon a rock, and established my goings."*
—Psalm 40:2 KJV

ACW Press
Ozark, AL 36360

Scripture quotations are taken from the King James Version of the Bible.

Out of the Miry Clay
Copyright ©2006 M.I. Scarrott
All rights reserved

Cover Photograph by Joshua K. Abbott © 2004
Cover Design by Alpha Advertising
Interior Design by Pine Hill Graphics

Packaged by ACW Press
1200 HWY 231 South #273
Ozark, AL 36360
www.acwpress.com
The views expressed or implied in this work do not necessarily reflect those of ACW Press. Ultimate design, content, and editorial accuracy of this work is the responsibility of the author(s).

Publisher's Cataloging-in-Publication Data
(Provided by Cassidy Cataloguing Services, Inc.)

Scarrott, M. I.

    Out of the miry clay : a novel / M. I. Scarrott. — 1st ed. — Ozark, AL : ACW Press, 2006.

      p. ; cm.

    ISBN-13: 978-1-932124-78-1
    ISBN-10: 1-932124-78-0

    1. Redemption—Fiction. 2. Faith—Fiction. 3. Spiritual life—Fiction. 4. Christian fiction. I. Title.

PS3569.C377 O88 2006
813.54—dc22   0604

Printed in the United States of America.

Thank you…

To my loving husband, Chuck, who has been a constant source of faithful support for thirty years.

To my daughter Michelle Abbott, who not only read through my manuscript but always encourages me while I write; she also posed for the cover of this book.

To my son-in-law Josh Abbott who is a steady man of faith and who also took the photograph for the cover of this book.

To my dear friends Eva Montgomery, Violeta Valladares and Linda Hornbek, who are all devoted and faithful friends who took the time to read this manuscript.

To all my dear prayer partners: men and women of God who prayed as I wrote.

Michelle and Josh Abbott, Eva Montgomery, Violeta and Julio Valladares, Linda Hornbek, Amy Kaylor, Bea Newman, Karen Packard, Cynthia Sanchez, Steve and Joanne Wood, Amy Stabe, and Peggy Stabe.

My prayer partners speak for the first time:
here is what they had to say.

We want to thank God for His constant protection and provision in our lives. Along our path, He has sent many Christian helpers and advisors to guide our way. We pray to one day be a blessing to others as they have blessed us.

—Josh and Michelle Abbott

I want to thank the Lord for the many ways He blesses me and my family. I also thank Him for my dear friend, Peggie, who through her teaching and writing inspires, encourages and speaks truth all for the glory of God.

—Eva Montgomery

There are many things that I should like to thank the Lord for. I am grateful that He has carried my family through difficult times and provided for us in the midst of what often seemed to be a disaster. We are always aware of His sweet presence, especially since He blesses us with a loving family and dear friends.

—Bea Newman

We want to express our thanks to God for His continued blessings, for throughout our lives we have felt His presence. And especially thanks for the blessing of having Peggie's friendship and for being able to learn so much and gain wisdom from her wonderful books. Praise God!

—Julio and Violeta Valladares

Having known Peggie as a Bible teacher and friend, it has been a delight to read the novels she wrote that put God's teachings into a woman's life journey. There are so many biblical truths explained in the story of Rachel Todd that I feel blessed to know the author!

—Amy Kaylor

Praise my Potter's hands for molding and making me for His purpose. And for Joe my husband and best friend—He matched us perfectly.

—Linda Hornbek

I would like to thank my heavenly Father for the gift of life, family, friends, salvation and eternal life. Thank you for loving me, Lord.

—Cynthia Sanchez

Thanks to God for His wonderful gift of saving faith in Jesus Christ; and Peggie's faithfulness in writing for the sake of the gospel.

—Karen Packard

.

Table of Contents

Chapter One

Birth Pangs

Myra Clayborn thought monochromatically. An injury sustained early in life had damaged her ability to see color in the world. Years of disappointment destroyed hopeful expectations and led her to the brink of despair where thoughts of death became her daily companions.

Deceitful promises spoken by whispering spirits offered easy solutions to end her desolation. Believing the lies she indulged in the pleasures guaranteed to secure the love she so desperately desired. Her pain subsided but only for a moment until a new wound appeared more vulgar than the first. The twisted truth had been the enemy's deception, which plunged her more deeply into darkness torturing her already tormented soul securing her captivity in seclusion more decisively, until…

Boom! Thunder clapped outside my window. I closed the book and laid it down on the table beside me to contemplate the meaning behind the mystery. Myra Clayborn's story was intriguing and inspirational, and thoughts of meeting her for the first time filled me with mixed feelings of delight and expectation. The fact that she had written the introduction to her history as an analogy was intriguing; and in a way it inexplicably compelled me to read on.

Myra had become a small but powerful voice speaking to the masses; human souls ready for harvest were like brands to be plucked from the fires of hell and this, she stated, was her earthly commission. She wanted to combat the strongholds of evil that had taken residence in the lives of people keeping them imprisoned in misery and despair.

January had been extremely cold and wet; fifteen inches of rain had already descended this season, eight in the past three weeks. We had already surpassed our annual level, which was something closer to twelve. The usual stories of mud slides and water damage filled the newspapers and the American Red Cross and Salvation Army were busy assisting those in need of temporary shelter and supplies.

A warm fire blazed nicely in the hearth of the large old fireplace situated in my sitting room, keeping the normally cool area cozy while the rain poured down outside. The wood being consumed by the flames was an awful reminder of Myra's words: *brands plucked from the fires of hell.*

I was enjoying my quiet morning alone; Martha had brought my breakfast in on a tray and while relaxing I sipped a cup of hot cranberry tea and nibbled on the crumbs of a hot, buttery scone until another crack of thunder awakened me from my contemplation.

I walked to the balcony and opened the doors; the ocean was barely visible today due to the weather. It was raining profusely so I closed the doors and shut the drapes to keep out the cold and then returned to my reading.

When the clock on the wall chimed nine I left the bedroom to take a shower; the steaming hot water gently awakened my body, rejuvenating it for the busy day ahead. My long auburn hair was already wrapped neatly in a tight chignon so after applying my makeup all I needed to do was dress.

My attire for the day was casual and chic but functional; a long hunter green woolen skirt with a matching bolero jacket worn with an ivory turtleneck sweater would keep me warm and dry if the rain continued. Black stockings and boots were fashionable accoutrements to my outfit and appropriate shields from the inclement weather. I surveyed myself in a long mirror and smiled—not bad for a grandmother!

Patricia was already in the foyer with my coat and hat when I descended the long winding stairway from my bedroom to the front hall. Patrick, her husband, was waiting with her carrying an umbrella. He opened the front door and together we stepped out into the rain; he escorted me to the car and I stepped inside next to Prudence, my friend and bodyguard. Sam, her associate, was at the helm.

We drove slowly down the estate driveway until we reached the highway; there, we cautiously joined the flowing traffic traveling more slowly than usual due to the heavy rain. Our trip lasted only fifteen minutes and we arrived without incident at our destination. Sam parked the car at the rear of the old brick building our church had recently purchased; we quickly left our vehicle and headed toward the rear entrance.

The lovely three-story brick building had been erected sometime in the late 1890s by a local rancher. Originally constructed as a hotel, it had been owned and operated by many for a variety of purposes during the last century, and was still in remarkable condition. It sat on a large corner lot in the middle of town near our small neighborhood church, which had grown considerably over the years, and had acquired the building for use as a school. Due to its age, it needed to be renovated before we could safely begin classes. Fortunately, one of our board members, an architect, had surveyed the property and was working with a contractor to make the necessary changes.

The ground floor consisted of a large meeting room, which we wanted to use for lectures and seminars, a large office, a kitchen and utility room and several small sitting rooms. The second and third floors had been hotel rooms that would be converted into classrooms; each floor had a private parlor and bathroom facilities that made it ideal for our purpose.

Sam, as a precaution, was the first to enter the building; I walked behind him and Prudence followed behind me. John and Sarah Edwards, our church pastors, had already arrived and greeted us warmly.

"Come in!" Sarah said sweetly, "Let me take your coats," she offered, holding out her hands.

"Thanks, Sarah," I replied removing my raincoat and handing it to her. "Is Myra here yet?" I asked anxiously.

"No, not yet. We expect her any minute though," Sarah responded politely.

"We'll be meeting in the principal's office," John said matter-of-factly. "It's a bit warmer in there and I believe the conference table will be large enough to accommodate our small party."

"That's fine," I replied and together we made our way down a long hallway toward the front of the building where the office was located near the front entrance. Nick Daniels, the pastor's administrative assistant, who had apparently been busy setting up the room, said hello as we entered and offered each of us a hot drink.

Walking into the long rectangular office was like stepping back in time; it was austere in a way but the room had an old-fashioned literary charm that I found irresistible. There was a large ornate fireplace in the middle of an exterior wall with a marble mantle. On either side of it were several high windows placed above a series of bookshelves; I thought it might have originally been a card room in days when it was a hotel or perhaps a library. Regardless, it was now generally referred to as the principal's office.

A large mahogany desk sat gracefully at one end of the room surrounded by large overstuffed chairs covered in burgundy leather. The long, wide table that occupied the area at the opposite end of the room was elaborate and beautiful; its sides and legs were hand carved with an exquisite design that reminded me greatly of my grandfather's work. He had been an exceptional carpenter and it was through him that I had gained the acumen to detect quality workmanship.

I took a seat at the table near John and Sarah and we chatted casually while we waited for our guests to arrive. Sam and Prudence positioned themselves at opposite ends of the room standing in silent vigilance as always.

Two large windows, at the front of the room, faced toward the town hall and police department, which were across the street. Several smaller windows lined the adjoining outside wall, which faced a side street that housed a number of small offices; the local fire department was one block down the same street.

The rain continued to pour nonstop as lightning flashed across the sky and the sound of thunder followed; God was making his voice heard intently today. It felt a bit eerie being in the old building, which creaked mysteriously around us, obviously from age and perhaps due in part to the dampness.

Voices emanating from the hallway announced the arrival of our guests; Pastor John and Sarah arose quickly from the table and walked to the back door to greet them; moments later four venerable ladies were ushered into the office. Laughter filled the air as they joyfully removed their wet coats and handed them to Nick, who gracefully carried them to the coat rack in the foyer so John and Sarah could rejoin us at the table.

Pastor John made the introductions and we greeted one another with warm affection and a sense of anticipation. I met Moira first; she was obviously the youngest member of this eclectic group and I guessed her to be approximately thirty years old. She was tall and thin with long red hair and she, we were told, was their musician. Laurel, closer to forty than thirty, was of medium height and had short brown hair. A lovely African-American woman, Laurel was an executive assistant to the CEO of a large construction company and handled all their travel arrangements. Elena, a short robust Latina woman in her mid to late fifties was a bi-lingual communications expert. I met Myra Clayborn, our honored guest, last. She was a short, stout, gray-haired woman of sixty; her brown eyes sparkled, she smiled sincerely and when she shook my hand firmly it was electric.

Tea, coffee and cookies were offered to the ladies as refreshment after their travels; the inclement weather made the hot beverage a delight and the chocolate-macadamia nut cookies, which Sarah had baked, were delectable.

John and Sarah Edwards had been close personal friends for many years, so I knew them quite well. He was the first to speak after the refreshments were served, introducing himself and sharing a bit of his vision for our small ocean-side community. A kind, sensitive and intelligent man, John had a heart for God and people; the greatest desire of his life was to see lost souls surrender their lives to God.

In doing so he believed their faith could inspire them to walk in hope while overcoming difficult situations in a spirit of love.

Myra, as an author and speaker, told us she used her gifts to promote a message, which she commonly summarized in three words: truth, trust and transformation. She said the novels she wrote were "contemporary parables" wherein she used fictional characters to teach the biblical values she so adamantly espoused. And while their visions were different their passion was the same and it prompted Sarah, who had met Myra the previous year, to consider engaging her as the guest speaker for our fall women's conference.

"Dear ladies," John began slowly, "we thank you for traveling so far in such bad weather to meet with us; we want you to know how much we appreciate your sacrifice and commitment." The ladies smiled and nodded and John continued. "Having read several of Myra's books I am able to speak about them from familiarity; they are thought provoking, inspirational and entertaining. And I believe they reveal the heart of their creator and her essential beliefs, which we share as well. Sarah and I are grateful for your willingness to be a part of our vision for our congregation and I want to thank you for allowing me to participate in your planning session." He then turned the meeting over to Sarah.

"It is with tremendous delight," she said, "that we welcome you to our small community church. We have been looking forward to this time together as it is our desire to get to know you better and pray for you as you prepare to minister to members of our congregation. During the past few months while we've been communicating, we believe a friendship between us has been birthed and that God will continue to develop it over time. As you already know, the theme of our conference is 'Standing upon the Rock,' and we are eager to hear the revelation you hope to share with those who plan to attend."

"I appreciate your kindness and your invitation," Myra began slowly and modestly. "We believe God has a purpose for us, and we endeavor to go wherever God seeks to send us. We are here today because we believe as you do that the Lord has a purpose for us in this lovely community.

"As you are already aware, I am not a professional speaker and what I share comes strictly from my heart. I never acquired a college degree nor am I a member of the clergy; my training comes from the Holy Spirit as does my ordination.

"I am just a simple woman; a plain earthborn vessel created for the Master's use. I think of myself as a plate designed to serve; the food I serve is the Bread of Life, and it is what nourishes and sustains hungry souls. The plate does not provide nourishment," she continued humbly, "it is only a receptacle so its value must be seen in its service—nothing more, nothing less."

Myra spoke softly, clearly, succinctly and with conviction and I found myself sincerely captivated by her humble demeanor and the simple way she expressed her beliefs; her words rang true and settled comfortably within my spirit.

Thunder clapped loudly outside, rattling the windows; the noise startled me and I jumped along with a few of the others who then smiled and laughed. "'The voice of the Lord is powerful,'" Myra said, quoting Psalms and then continued speaking in metaphors referring to herself as a simple work of clay, an object of the earth designed to speak earthy but profound words to a lost world. She shared just a snippet of her own story with us and the gratitude she felt at being called out of darkness into the light of Christ's love; her story was one of resurrection, her journey a source of encouragement, her meekness genuine and inspiring.

A bright light flashed across the sky, illuminating the room, and the rumble of thunder quickly followed. This time, however, the earth began to move and shake, quickly growing in intensity and magnitude.

"Earthquake!" Sam yelled from his silent post near the door. "Get under the table." Quickly, we pushed aside our chairs and sought shelter under the immense old table, the only place where we could be safe from falling objects. Huddled close together, the room continued to move and sway; within seconds we were bathed in murky darkness. The noise of the earth's roar was deafening; I could hear the sound of broken glass but kept my eyes covered and my head tucked closely to my body. The air became heavily saturated with dirt, dust and debris, evidence the building was failing in places. The table overhead shook as the ground rolled beneath us and the sound of heavy objects falling added to my fears; I quietly prayed the ceiling wouldn't collapse on top of us.

The temblor lasted a little less than thirty seconds but the damage done in that short span of time was often immeasurable. When the earth finally stopped moving, I found myself frozen in fear, clutching one leg of the enormous table. We all remained still for a matter of moments until we were reasonably sure the quake was over. Slowly we climbed out from under our safe haven to view the wreckage.

The only light in the room streamed from the open windows, many of which were now bereft of glass. Prudence, who had sought refuge near me, quickly looked around the room, calling each person by name. John, Sarah and Nick were fine. Elena, Laurel and Moira were all fine. Sam and Myra were covered in dirt but were uninjured as well. They were at the other end of the table, closest to the corner wall.

"We probably should go outside," Sam suggested. "I'm not sure about the integrity of this building; it may not withstand an aftershock, which is sure to follow."

"I agree," John Edwards said and we began to exit the building as quickly as possible. "Be careful where you walk," John said leading the way, "portions of the ceiling have fallen." We stepped cautiously as we walked toward the back doors, trying to avoid tripping and falling over any of the debris. Just as we reached the rear door of the building the earth began to shake violently again. We crouched into archways waiting for it to end; when it did we made our way quickly outside where we could maneuver freely. Looking around the parking lot Prudence began to count heads again.

"Where's Myra?" Laurel asked fearfully.

"She and Sam were together," Pastor Edwards said as he turned around and went back into the building, Nick following close behind. Several long minutes later he and Nick reemerged carrying Myra in their arms; her leg was bleeding profusely. Laurel opened the back door of her SUV so they could lay Myra down inside; Sam had followed the trio outside and quickly made his way to the car to retrieve the first aid kit and a blanket.

"Rubble from the back of the building has blocked the entrance to the parking lot," Nick said, looking for a way out.

"Call 911!" John said quickly.

"They're bound to be swamped with calls," Sam replied, "even if you can get through."

"The fire department's just up the road; I'll go for help," Nick said and he turned and quickly ran down the street. Prudence wrapped Myra's leg to stop the bleeding as much as possible and then covered her with the blanket while the rest of us began to remove what debris we could to free the passageway out of the parking lot. It seemed like only minutes had passed before we heard the wail of a siren announcing the arrival of the paramedics.

The rain had slowed to a mist fortunately, but we were soaking wet regardless; our coats were lost somewhere inside the building and we were beginning to grow cold. Myra was placed on a stretcher and lifted into the back of an ambulance, which was now screaming down the highway toward the hospital.

Sam looked miserable watching the ambulance as it disappeared down the street.

"It isn't your fault!" I said hastily.

"We were just walking out the door when the aftershock struck. Myra was a few steps ahead of me; a loose portion of the ceiling must have given way and dropped down on top of her. There was nothing I could do to protect her," he said painfully.

"We need to go to the hospital to be with Myra," Elena said, redirecting our attention to the difficulty at hand. It took a while but the men working together were finally able to push the largest pieces of debris away to make a large enough opening so we could leave.

"We'll go with you," I offered quickly, "at least to show you the way."

John locked the door of the school and then he, Sarah and Nick departed. They needed to go to the church to open it for those who might need shelter, aid or counseling.

Prudence, Sam and I escorted Myra's team to the hospital and after promising to check back with them to see about her condition, we began our drive home. We tuned the radio to a local station to receive the news reports about the earthquake; there was a great deal of speculation over the magnitude, but those of us who had experienced other temblors predicted it would be around a six.

Our community had a very good emergency preparedness

plan, which comprised several teams we knew would already be assembling; Noah, my business manager, headed the team for our area.

On the journey home we were able to survey some of the damage in town, which appeared minimal. I felt relieved when we turned off the highway and onto the road that led to the estate entrance; it too appeared intact. Grandfather had built his home well; the strong structure had survived several natural disasters over the years and had been through a number of very strong earthquakes suffering only minimal damage.

We made a quick stop at the Tea Cottage to speak to Noah before going up the hill; his team members were already arriving and preparing to depart to perform their designated tasks.

"Have you spoken to Miriam? Is everyone at Tabitha's House okay?" I asked hastily.

"Yes, they're fine. I had to use the walkie-talkies; the telephone lines are out and the cell phones are constantly busy. I've already spoken to Eli too. It seems the earthquake didn't do that much damage in our area; I heard the epicenter was approximately fifty miles to the north of us."

"John Edwards is setting up the church as an emergency shelter; if people need crisis counseling you can send them there. Please check with him when you have a chance to see if he needs anything. And if any of our staff members live in the quake area or need to leave, let them go. Those who can stay should begin to prepare food for the emergency workers."

"Don't worry, Rachel; we're already on board," Noah said with a smile.

I thanked Noah and after checking in with Sophie at the Victorian Inn next to the Tea Cottage, we drove up the hill toward home.

When I entered the front foyer of the estate I was greeted by Patricia carrying Baby, my toy poodle, who was shaking in fear.

"Is everyone okay?" I asked, quickly taking the dog from her.

"Yes," she replied anxiously. "We had some breakage in several of the rooms upstairs and a few broken windows. Patrick has the grounds crew checking every room and he's inspecting the secret passageway and the basement himself."

"Thank you. Patricia. You look like you need a cup of tea. Why don't you join me?" I said and we walked to the kitchen to see Martha.

"Mum," she said when we walked through the doorway, "I was so worried about ya!" I walked over to Martha and gave her a big hug.

"I'm fine, Martha. Are you all right?"

"I'm fine," she replied stoically. "It was a real shaker, wasn't it?" she said with a laugh. "Lost some of my favorite bowls though," she wailed in her thick Irish brogue.

"Don't worry, they can be replaced. I'm happy that no one was hurt. Have you heard from Christopher?"

"No, Mum. The telephone isn't working."

"I tried to call him on my cell phone but the circuits are busy," I complained. "He'll get through when he can, I'm sure. I'm going to take a hot shower and change my clothes to get the dust out of my face and hair. Patricia needs a cup of tea," I said looking at Martha who shook her head and put the kettle on and then sat down to take care of her frightened friend.

Christopher, my husband, was still in London, settling his parents' estate. Morgan, his father, died suddenly after suffering from a heart attack; his mother Clare went just a few weeks later after succumbing to pneumonia. They were together on earth for more than half a century; now they were walking on streets of gold.

The power was out but the estate was equipped with emergency generators to handle all of our energy needs. I showered quickly, changed my clothes and hurried downstairs with Baby, not wanting to be alone if another aftershock hit.

Martha made dinner for our household and the grounds crew was sent down the hill to eat at the Tea Cottage with other emergency workers and their teams. News reports coming over the radio reported the quake's magnitude at 5.8; the epicenter was as previously stated, about fifty miles north of our location.

When Noah arrived later that night he brought good news regarding the community, which was in comparatively good shape. The majority of damage done appeared to be in the older buildings whose structures hadn't been retrofitted to meet current earthquake standards. Losses in areas closer to the epicenter were more significant but fortunately we had been spared. The Red Cross had set up a shelter in the local high school and the Church of the Open Door would be open all day and night to help those in need, assisted by the Salvation Army and its dedicated staff.

Several aftershocks shook the estate that evening but each was considerably smaller and of shorter duration than those before. I hesitated to go to sleep but weary after the stressful events of the day I finally dozed off sometime after two in the morning. When I awoke the next day the storm had passed, the sun was shining and the birds were once again singing gay melodies outside my balcony window.

Feeling famished I dressed quickly and hurried downstairs to get a bite to eat. Martha had bacon, eggs and potatoes O'Brien on the stove when I arrived and after pouring myself a cup of steaming black coffee, I devoured the scrumptious meal she had prepared. Prudence was just coming on duty and after she finished eating her breakfast I told her I wanted to drive into town to see Myra. She quietly left the room in search of Patrick who would bring the car around; Sam and she would accompany me as usual.

In less than an hour we arrived at the hospital where Myra Clayborn was now a patient. Laurel, Elena and Moira had spent the evening in the waiting room concerned about the welfare of their friend. They told me she had a mild concussion from a blow she received to the side of her head, an injury no one had noticed the day before. She was also in a great deal of pain due to a shattered leg, which would require surgery. She was going to be transferred first, however, to a larger hospital nearer her home.

I entered Myra's room quietly fearing she might still be asleep but as I drew near to her bed she opened her eyes and smiled.

"Ah, Rachel, it's so good of you to come today," she said sweetly.

"Myra," I said taking hold of her hand, "how are you?" I asked tearfully.

"Fine," she assured. "Please don't worry about me."

"I'm just so terribly sorry that you were injured," I exclaimed regretfully.

"We mustn't question what God allows," was her sweet response. Myra then closed her eyes; I sensed she might be in pain but I waited silently for her to speak again. When she did, her voice was barely audible; she said almost in a whisper, "The earth is groaning, Rachel...I believe it's the beginning of birth pangs."

Chapter Two

A Global Warning

*T*he brief conversation we shared that morning still burned in my mind; Myra's thought-provoking comments were strangely prophetic and almost frightening. While many people simply accepted "natural disasters" as the workings of "Mother Nature" we believed otherwise. "God controls the weather; he is the real force behind the global disasters that are occurring with greater frequency and ferocity," she went on to say that morning in the hospital. "We're living in the end times, Rachel; and God is sending us a very critical message!" I knew she was right.

Christopher, ever the pragmatist, made arrangements to fly home immediately when word of the earthquake reached him. A gentle man of quiet strength and action, he knew instinctively where to focus his attention in order to do the most good. Personally, it was a great relief just having him home.

The first two weeks after the catastrophe were the most difficult; we watched the news incessantly as reports came in on a daily basis updating the statistics on fatalities and disaster damage, which sometimes changed minute by minute. My heart ached for those who had lost loved ones; I knew their lives would be changed forever. Although material losses were significant, things, unlike people, could be replaced.

Myra and I kept in close contact speaking by telephone often once she was moved to a hospital closer to home; our initial meeting had been brief but we had connected and formed a bond, which I hoped would flourish over time. Her leg surgery to repair her shattered bones went well and although she would be confined for some months, she was grateful, as were we, that her injuries weren't more severe.

Myra was a bit mysterious but extremely interesting; when I spoke of her to Chris I realized how tremendously intrigued I was by her deeply passionate personality. In a day when so many leaders appeared arrogant and untrustworthy it was a pleasure to meet someone so completely humble and yet direct; as I grew to know and understand her better I began to believe her lack of degreed education had been a blessing instead of a curse.

One evening while Chris and I sat alone in the parlor reading and then talking, I shared a portion of a recent conversation with Myra in which she explained a particularly difficult theodicy; I considered it an interesting revelation.

"Myra laughed at me when I commented on the depths of her wisdom," I said smiling. "She simply replied that anyone who listens to and obeys the word of God is wise."

Christopher grinned. "She does sound like a very astute woman; I can't wait to meet her," he said enthused. "You mentioned that she said the increased frequency of natural disasters occurring around the world is prophetic; the beginning of birth pangs?" he asked rather abruptly.

"Yes, that's what she said. Why?"

"Well, I've just been reading an article in this news magazine about that very subject: natural disasters. I'm afraid the author doesn't agree however," he said raising his eyebrows just a bit and smiling. It was raining again and colder than normal outside and we were enjoying the warmth and glow of the fire burning on the hearth, but it was growing dim. Before continuing our conversation Chris got up and threw a few small logs on the fire and stirred up the remains of a log that had almost been consumed. He returned to his place on the sofa next to me and continued.

"What does it say?" I asked intrigued. "The article," I added pointing to his magazine.

"Well, they do concur with Myra's estimation that natural disasters are increasing globally." My heart rate sped up dramatically as he read portions of the article detailing the statistics out loud. "The author writes about tornadoes ripping through America's heartland, massive floods and mudslides, wildfires and volcanic eruptions and the increase in typhoons and hurricanes, and of course the recent tsunami, just to give a few examples as evidence of the increase."

"And what do they attribute all these things to?" I asked sardonically. "Oh, wait, let me guess: global warming!" I said.

"Exactly!" he answered again with a charismatic grin.

"That figures, doesn't it?" I asked.

"Yes, because the natural man looks to the scientific community for answers rather than God. But I agree with Myra, and what scientific men attribute to global warming, I believe is really a 'global warning.' "

"Birth pangs!" I said, reiterating Myra's words.

"Yes, birth pangs. God is trying to get our attention. As our national sin increases, so do natural disasters," he replied. Chris set the magazine down on the coffee table next to him. "Just look at the past decade, Rachel. This nation has been experiencing some of the worst weather in its history. Global warming is a fact; the earth is getting hotter and much of the land is getting drier, which will, I'm afraid, eventually lead to massive famine and starvation; another prophecy. We simply won't be able to grow the food we'll need to survive; it is *apocalyptic*."

"And frightening!" I said almost in a whisper.

"The violent extremes we've been experiencing in the weather will grow worse and science won't be able to stop it," Chris said meditatively. "The only hope for mankind is repentance; if we repent, perhaps God will show mercy. If not, then I'm afraid that we really are teetering on the brink of the end of civilization."

"People rarely repent when tragedy happens, Chris, you know that. They usually get angry at God instead and blame him for their grief," I said, somewhat dispirited.

"Yes, I'm afraid you're right, Darling." He took my hand and drew it to his mouth and kissed it gently. "Knowledge can at times be a bit overwhelming, can't it?" he asked. "But we mustn't worry; we need to trust that God knows what he's doing!"

"I know; it does scare me though." I sat silently not moving a muscle; were we really facing the end of the world? Sadness filled my heart as my mind raced in a million different directions; was our country really so terribly corrupt?

"How is a nation corrupted, Chris?" I asked inquisitively. "I mean how did we get here?"

"How?" he responded repeating my question. "How is a nation corrupted? That's a fairly complex question," he said thoughtfully and sitting back into the arm of the sofa he began to ponder the problem to formulate a response.

"Corruption equals decay or decomposition so basically it occurs when something within begins to break down," he began somewhat systematically. "Corruption is a consequence of depravity; it results when we turn away from what is moral and good. Corrupt people usually have an impaired sense of integrity or none at all; they have no moral compass.

"This nation is a democracy 'of the people, by the people and for the people': it is therefore the people that determine who and what will govern them. So, the people are, to a great extent, responsible for the moral integrity of the land.

"If the people elect moral men and women of virtue and integrity, the nation will flourish; if they elect immoral individuals the nation will perish. Healthy trees produce healthy fruit; and that old adage about one bad apple spoiling the barrel is actually true.

"Immoral societies erode from within and in time they expire," he said solemnly. "People are more selfish than ever and because they are, evil flourishes."

"That's truer than you know; selfishness is rampant. People living for no one but themselves; and since their allegiance is to their appetites they reject anyone or anything that seeks to prick their conscience. They want us to believe that black is white and white is black; it's almost as if they're imbued with a spirit of rebellion."

Chris gave me a funny look and then agreed. "You're right, a spirit of rebellion is at work. Consider the current campaign being waged by modern secularists; they are engaged in a calculated crusade to rid the nation and its government of all vestiges of religion. Why? So every man can do whatever he wants: that is a spirit of rebellion at work.

"Secularism is being welcomed by a great number of people, but in my opinion, it's simply the Trojan horse that will destroy this nation if it continues to gain ground. Secularists claim God has no place in our modern legal system and therefore they seek to remove him, and his commandments, from the land. And then they wonder why there are so many problems in public schoolrooms."

"No commandments; no restrictions: everything goes. It's insane!"

"And what too few realize is that the Ten Commandments were used by England to form its common law, which the United States followed; this country was established on Judeo-Christian ethics. If this nation wants to continue to enjoy freedom and justice, then it needs to return to its biblical roots; perhaps then God will restore the land to health. If not…"

We talked for some time sharing our thoughts about current events and the moral demise of the nation and when we finally retired for the night, I was too restless to sleep.

Grandfather's old clock sitting on the mantle ticked away the minutes of the hour while Chris's words echoed in my mind. I closed my eyes and tried to drown out my thoughts but the tick, tick, ticking of the clock reminded me that time was passing quickly. The alarm was sounding but few were listening; I feared the inevitable would happen when our time finally ran out.

Chapter Three

Valentine's Day

February 14, St. Valentine's Day, was our anniversary. In order to commemorate the day, we were giving a small dinner party and had invited only family and close friends to attend. The years had breezed by like days filled with sunshine and rain. We had weathered some difficult storms together but nothing had been able to detour us from our path of devotion. We were soul mates, inseparable and very much in love.

Chris was a traditionalist so I knew he would bring me candy or flowers to celebrate the day; most likely there would be roses: white roses or pink roses, maybe even yellow roses and lilies. There wouldn't be red roses…no, sadly enough, there would never again be red roses. Not since the mystery of the surreptitious stalker had been solved had there been red roses in our home; they evoked too many painful memories. In their place there would be something else, something truly sterling; something uniquely particular, an extraordinary gift from his heart to mine.

Our marriage was what I thought all marriages should be: a mystical union between two souls, a commitment between two hearts, and a contract of faithfulness lived out in the presence of God and blessed particularly by him because we were devoted.

On Valentine's morning I awoke to the sounds of Puccini; a beautiful rendition of "Nessun Dorma" emanated from the stereo. A tall, thin vase with three long-stemmed sterling roses was sitting on my nightstand, a diamond necklace dripping from its verdant green leaves. I smiled and removed the necklace from its leafy green perch to admire it. A diamond-shaped diamond was placed in the center and formed the point of the heart; two round-shaped rubies filled out the top; it was breathtaking. A note attached to the vase written in Chris's hand read: *And the two shall become one. Happy Anniversary, Darling!*

I looked around the room and uttered his name softly but my "dear boy" was nowhere to be seen, so I called down to the kitchen to speak to Martha.

"Your husband went out on an errand, Mum. He told me to bring ya your heart's delight for breakfast; he wasn't sure how long it might be before he returns."

I asked Martha to make me a Belgian waffle covered with strawberries and whipped cream and she complied and served it with a steaming hot pot of vanilla tea. I quickly devoured my breakfast with joy savoring every morsel. I read for awhile and then prayed before showering and getting dressed. My feet fairly flew down the stairs with elation knowing the family would soon be home for the weekend.

"He hasn't returned yet?" I asked Martha as I entered the kitchen, headquarters of her earthly domain, where she reigned as Queen Supreme, and an Irish one at that!

"No, Mum!" she quickly replied. "And he didn't tell me where he was off to! I only know he left in a hurry and had that determined look on his face that he often gets when he's on a mission of importance."

I laughed out loud; I too knew that look.

"Breakfast was delightful," I said to my friend and companion. "I'm going for a walk down the hill to the Inn and then over to the Cottage," I said and taking a hat and jacket in hand I made my way toward the front door. Prudence, my bodyguard, quietly traced my steps and in no time at all we were on the path that led to the Victorian bed and breakfast we owned down below.

It was cold outside; the air was delightfully crisp and the blue sky was dazzling; I was thankful that it wasn't raining. The earth was overly saturated from the heavy winter rainfall and several hills and mountains had collapsed as a result. An abundance of communities had suffered horrible losses when floods of dark brown mud covered their homes; it was devastating to see how quickly the earth could slide, moving a mountain erasing every trace of humanity with it.

Sophie, the manager of the inn, was in her office located on the third floor when I arrived.

"Good morning!" I said in a cheery greeting as I knocked on her door.

"Good morning and Happy Anniversary!" she replied with enthusiasm.

"Thank you!" I replied and then added, "Is everything set for the weekend?" I was sure it would be; Sophie was an incredible administrator but I asked regardless.

"Yes, it is!" she replied with a smile. "Every room has a bowl of fresh flowers and a basket of ripe fruit, just as you requested," she added with a smile.

Most of our weekend guests would be staying at the estate along with the family but a few "outsiders" would be housed at the inn, which was closed to the public during this festive occasion.

"Next week, we need to meet to discuss room renovations," I said sitting down in one of the large chairs she kept for visitors. "I really liked the ideas you submitted for redecorating too," I added. "I've been toying with your proposal to add a conservatory to the back of the inn just like we did at Sweet Dreams."

"Oh, Rachel, thanks. I think it would be a wonderful addition!" Sophie exclaimed.

"I may need to put it off for a while; people are pretty busy rebuilding after the earthquake. And Patrick told me we may need to do some work on the estate; he found some problems in the basement area we've yet to fully discuss. We'll see," I promised and after finishing our business I said good-bye and walked over to the Tea Cottage.

Noah was busy speaking to the host positioned at the front door work station when I entered the restaurant. I found an empty table in one of the converted stalls and seated myself; a server brought me a cup of tea and when Noah was finished with his conversation, he joined me at my table. We exchanged a few casual pleasantries before he took the time to assure me that Chris's anniversary gift would be delivered on time and as planned.

"The Cottage is quiet this morning," I said after we concluded our business. The orange spice tea I had requested from the waiter was delicious.

"Business has been affected by some recent road closures," Noah responded by way of explanation. "There were several severe mud slides up the coast, which closed some of the local access roads but I believe they'll be open by Monday."

His comments concerned me; I knew most of our weekend guests would be coming up from the south but there were a few, Victoria included, who were driving down from the north.

"Perhaps I should call Victoria," I said thinking out loud.

"Don't worry, Rachel," Noah said reassuringly. "I checked this morning; she'll be able to get through," he said with a smile and after offering my thanks, I left the cottage to return home.

While walking up the long winding pathway toward the estate I saw Christopher's car drive through the security gate and up the road that led to our home. I was almost at the top of the hill when he jumped out of the car and hurried into the house carrying a small brown package in his hands. *Was this my mysterious gift?* I wondered.

Our daughters and their families along with our guests arrived at different intervals throughout the day raising the noise level of the house considerably. The hallways overflowed with the hearty laughter of children; their delightful squeals of joy were both enchanting and sonorous.

Caitlin Rose, now nearly three, was the apple of her grandfather's eye. She had bright red hair and soft green eyes that lit up her pale pink skin dotted with a smattering of tiny brown freckles. She called Chris "Poppy" and he called her "Caty Rose."

Chloe, Chris's only biological child by his first wife, was a petite woman with dark auburn brown hair and eyes. And even though she and Charlotte were stepsisters, they looked a great deal alike. She and her husband Scott were living happily in a suburb of Los Angeles just off Sunset Boulevard not too far from my daughter, Devon. Scott was still working for a cable news network that had brought them home to California; she was a happy homemaker.

My daughters, Victoria, Devon and Charlotte, were the progeny of my first marriage to Paul Todd, who had left me for a younger woman after almost three decades of marriage. Those painful days were now only a blur, a part of the history of my life's journey. A garment of praise had replaced the spirit of heaviness that once lingered over me. Christopher's kindness had reopened my closed and aching heart as he patiently blew out the ashes of mourning and filled it with the beauty of his love.

Dinner was scheduled for seven that evening. The children were all given a late snack to stave off hunger as they were to be included in all the evening festivities.

When the bells began to peal at six o'clock, our guests eagerly found their way to the small chapel located to the rear of the large family estate Chris and I inhabited. Once they were seated, Chris and I entered through the double oak doors, arm in arm, and walked to the altar at the front of the octagonal building. There, in the presence of our family and friends, we renewed our wedding vows and sealed them with a kiss.

The ballroom was decorated in resplendent shades of purple and light gray this evening, graciously complementing our attire. Chris was dressed in a pearl gray suit; I wore a lilac silk dress with pale lavender roses woven into the fabric; the bodice clung tightly to my body while the long skirt and train flowed freely behind.

Hannah Moore, who had been the flower girl at our wedding years before, was among the first of our friends to greet us after we left the chapel. She was now a stunning college beauty engaged to Adam Marshall, the eldest son of my best friend Marie. Her platinum blonde hair had darkened over the years and it was now a light golden color, which complemented her peachy complexion and crystal clear blue eyes. Miriam, her mother, and Noah Adams, her adopted father, had been my business associates and close personal friends for many years.

Chris and I stood together at the entrance to the ballroom

greeting each person as they came in and made their way to their dinner table. Charlotte, my youngest daughter, had long auburn hair and hazel eyes and although she was taller, she looked more like me than either of the other girls. She and Edgar and their children gave each of us a kiss as they entered; the twins, Eliza and E.J. were tall and thin; Ethan, the baby, had a heavier frame and was still a little on the chubby side.

Devon, my middle daughter, was a blue-eyed blonde like her father. She and Dari came in holding hands and wearing matching dresses. Mary, Dari's nanny and Martha's sister, we were told, was busy working side by side with her sibling in the kitchen, much to my chagrin. They were supposed to be taking the evening off to enjoy the festivities.

Victoria, my eldest daughter, looked a great deal like my grandmother had when she was young. Her round face sparkled with two large dimples and her chin-length strawberry blonde hair perfectly suited her strong bubbly personality. She and her philosopher husband Allen followed behind their sons, Michael and Riley, who took the lead. The boys wanted to be the first in their family to greet their grandparents with blessings and good wishes; my they were getting tall just like their father.

Chloe and Scott carried Caty Rose in after all the other guests had been greeted so her Poppy could carry her around on his shoulders, her favorite place to be.

Dinner was a sumptuous feast; the seafood buffet we had ordered was relished by all. There was lobster, cracked crab, shrimp, mussels, clams and oysters with a variety of side dishes. A string quartet entertained us while we dined and then a livelier band took over to play music for dancing. Prior to cutting our cake, Charlotte and Edgar performed a familiar duet: she on the piano and he on the cello. It was "The Swan" from *The Carnival of the Animals* by Camille Saint-Saëns; one of our favorites.

Christopher and I shared a small piece of cake and then danced to the "Anniversary Waltz" and at our invitation the dance floor filled with numerous couples enjoying the music. The ballroom buzzed all evening with lighthearted conversation and merriment; it warmed my heart to be blessed with such gentle companions.

When the band took a break, Chris walked up to the microphone to make an announcement; the room became remarkably quiet as soon as he began to speak.

"Rachel and I would like to thank you for coming this evening to celebrate our anniversary," he began soulfully. "We are extremely grateful to all of our friends who bless us with their love, companionship and faithfulness and to show our gratitude we would like to give you all something special to mark this extraordinary evening; we pray it will be a constant reminder of our affection for you." Chris then nodded to Noah who retrieved a gift-laden cart from the hallway and wheeled it into the center of the room. It was covered with small pink packages for the ladies and blue ones for the gentlemen; they all received diamond studded watches.

Standing close by my husband I joined him at the microphone to convey my appreciation to our guests.

"I also want to offer my thanks to you our dear friends for sharing our anniversary tonight. And while we are together, I would like you to share in my particular joy as I present a very special gift to a very special man," I said tenderly and taking one of Chris's hands into my own I gingerly placed a small rectangular box in his open palm. "This is for you, my darling!" I said and then gave him a kiss. Christopher grinned and looking somewhat mystified he shook the package slightly evoking laughter from those around us. We all watched anxiously when he finally began to remove the wrapping from the small foil package; he pulled open the box and then removed a key from inside. As he did, two young men standing at the ballroom doors opened them simultaneously while Noah switched on the outdoor lights. There parked on the edge of the patio terrace was a dazzling silver Ford GT with black racing stripes; I was told it could do 212 miles per hour.

"Happy Anniversary, Darling!" I said, ecstatic over his surprise.

"Rachel, I'm astounded!" he said giving me a hearty squeeze and a kiss.

"Hey, Dad, can I take it for a drive?" Scott said with a laugh, heading toward the door.

"Wait, please, everyone," Chris began. "Before we go outside to see my stunning new car…please, take a seat for a moment." Everyone was chattering amongst themselves but quickly returned to their seats.

"I have a very special gift to give to a very special lady as well," he began, retrieving a small package from his pocket lapel.

"While I was in England taking care of my parents' estate, I flew over to Paris to meet with an old friend; his name is Maurice and he has been a chemist most of his life. Today, he specializes in customizing perfumes for a very special clientele. I wanted to give Rachel something unique for our anniversary this year, so I went to Maurice and gave him a detailed description of my wife. I asked him to make a scent to match it," he exclaimed. "This is what I told him:

"Rachel is a delicate but strong woman; she is forceful but sensitive; loving but honest; truthful but diplomatic. She is as elegant as a rose; as innocent as a daisy; virtuous like the lily. She's as modest as a violet and as dignified as a magnolia.

"Rachel is a true woman of God; she is trustworthy, industrious, faithful and wise. I'm blessed to have her as my best friend, thankful for her love and devotion and proud to be called her husband.

"Maurice, who designed this perfume especially for her, also chose its name. He calls it 'Fidelity.'"

Christopher then handed me a small crystal vial of deep purple liquid. Tears of joy slipped silently down my cheeks and disappeared like magic into my already conquered heart.

⌐ *Chapter Four* ⌐

The Fragrance of Love

Christopher had watched with awe when the Ford GT 40 scored a historic win at the 1966 24 Hours of Le Mans; it was on a rainy day in June, one he would never forget. The Mark IIs took the first, second and third place positions and broke Ferrari's domination of the fast-paced endurance race. The GT 40 proved to be one of the fastest sports cars of its time when it went on to win at Le Mans again in 1967, 1968 and 1969.

The exotic Ford GT that I purchased for my husband wasn't an exact replica of the GT 40; this car was four inches taller and eighteen inches longer, and had been designed to make the cockpit roomier. It was an extravagant gift costing more than two hundred thousand dollars, and it needed to be pampered so it ran on premium gasoline. Mileage around town was about thirteen miles to the gallon; twenty-one perhaps on the highway.

People would be critical of my decision to purchase something so costly; they often were without just cause. Not knowing the full details behind a decision it was easy to be censorious; I hated to admit that there were times I had been guilty of the same injustice, a mistake I sincerely endeavored to correct.

It was after two in the morning when we finally retired for the evening; most of our guests had gone to bed as well; a few were still talking quietly in the parlor when we ascended the stairway to our room. The long day drew to a lovely end when I placed my vial of perfume on my dressing room table and Chris deposited the key to his new car delicately next to it; we then turned out the lights and went to bed.

We arose early the following morning to enjoy a hearty breakfast with our friends before making our way outdoors to take Christopher's new toy out for a little spin.

"There are only two seats!" I said to Prudence, climbing into the passenger side of the car next to my husband. "You needn't worry!" I remonstrated. "This baby can go from 0 to 60 miles per hour in 3.8 seconds; it's *incredibly* fast!" I snuggled into the leather seat, closed the door and waved good-bye to our family. Chris headed the Ford GT down the long, winding driveway toward the Pacific Ocean; we noticed several photographers positioned along the highway across the street from the entrance to the estate eagerly waiting to take pictures of whoever might emerge. I waved as we drove by laughing enthusiastically; nothing they could say or do could bother me today.

"Freedom is wonderful!" I cried to my husband who nodded in agreement as we purred along the coast highway; he was diligently obeying all traffic speed laws, which wasn't easy considering the GT's capability.

"Rachel, the car is fantastic," Chris said for the hundredth time. "This is really a dream come true!" he said energized by his new toy.

"Darling, I'm glad you like it," I replied softly.

"I know it's a short-lived delight but it's wonderful nonetheless. You know you'll be criticized in the press for being so extravagant!" he said with concern while grinning widely.

"Only our enemies will criticize us, not our friends," I quickly replied. "I refuse to be denied the opportunity to be generous and kind to one who is always so generous and kind; I wanted to give you something genuinely spectacular; even if you can only enjoy it for a little while," I replied to my loving husband. "Were you really surprised?" I asked.

"Completely!" he replied. "I expected something large because you said you were going to purchase something incredible that we could donate to the charity auction later this year, but I never dreamed it would be this," he said with enthusiasm.

"I'm glad!" I replied with a Cheshire grin. "And you'll get to enjoy it until then, my love."

Chris drove for a while and then pulled into a turnout so we could sit and watch the ocean and its beautiful billowing waves. He turned in his seat to face me; then taking my hand into his he said, "Rachel, your love reminds me of a fragrant ointment; it's a restorative balm to a weary man's soul; it is an agent of healing on days when life is difficult and a refreshing perfume when the atmosphere one breathes is laden with distress."

"Darling, you're always so poetic; I only wish I could find words adequate enough to tell you how much I love you. You have redeemed my life, Christopher, therefore it belongs to you."

He leaned across the seat and kissed my lips with such tenderness I almost cried.

"We better head for home now," he said quietly.

"Well, it was fun while it lasted," I said with a sigh. "I'm almost positive several members of our family will be anxiously awaiting our return," I laughed lightheartedly.

"Waiting for a ride, you mean," he quickly said as we made our way down the highway. When we finally pulled up to the front of the house, Scott and Edgar and several of the children were waiting outside, all anxious to try Grandpa's new car. Chris lightly tossed the keys to Scott, his son-in-law.

"Take it for a spin," Chris yelled, "but be careful, it's only mine for a while!"

Scott climbed inside the GT and Michael, our oldest grandson, climbed in next to him. In no time at all they disappeared from view. Christopher and I joined the others who were relaxing outside while the children played in the play yard.

"Great party last night, Mom," Charlotte said while pushing two of the girls on the swing set.

"It was a lot of fun," Victoria chimed in. "But I ate too much."

"Me too," Devon agreed. "Would you like a cup of coffee, Mom?" she asked and when I nodded she poured a cup from the thermal pot Patricia had brought outdoors.

"Are you really donating the car to charity?" Edgar asked in anguish.

"Yes, we really are, Ed. You know every year we have a huge summer charity auction and we always purchase something phenomenal to donate."

"And this year's auction is incredibly important," Christopher added, "because the onslaught of natural disasters that have occurred around the world has put a tremendous strain on the coffers of numerous charity organizations."

"The sale of the Ford GT should bring out some large donors; especially since I promised Chris would hand deliver it."

"Scott's back!" Edgar cried and headed toward the driveway for his chance to drive the GT; accompanied by E.J., his son, they took the next turn.

We were all enjoying the day outdoors; Martha, assisted by her sibling Mary, eventually brought lunch and snacks for us to eat and enjoy. Chris was busy talking to the men about the performance of the car while devouring a chicken salad sandwich; I chose egg salad and sat with the girls and their children.

People said that Providence had been good to us; I agreed. People even said that Providence had brought Chris and me together; I agreed with that as well. People called Providence fate; I did not. I called Providence divine intervention, and divine intervention when it occurred was often extremely amazing.

The children were playing happily together and my daughters were quietly conversing while my mind pleasantly drifted back to the first time Chris and I met. It was hard to believe that Juliet, his deceased wife, had been the instrument God used to bring us together.

Juliet had been a tireless fundraiser; she worked vigorously raising money for cancer research, a disease she fought so hard to eradicate but eventually succumbed to. We had known each other casually but I had never met her famous movie star husband, although I knew who he was. After she passed, he decided to step in and take her place and sought me out to help. At the time, neither he nor I was interested in forming any romantic attachments but we grew to be good friends and eventually we fell in love and married. We had been working diligently to aid a number of causes ever since.

Celebrity auctions were nothing new; many entertainers and icons used their VIP status to raise funds for charity; Chris and I were no different. The Ford GT by itself would raise a considerable amount of money, but a Ford GT previously owned by an Academy Award winning actor of Christopher's reputation would bring much, much more, especially when the handsome man agreed to deliver it in person!

The charity auction was scheduled for Labor Day weekend, and the bidding on the Ford GT would begin at five hundred thousand dollars. Until then, it belonged to Christopher, and I wanted him to enjoy it.

His real anniversary gift from me was a portrait of his parents I had commissioned a local artist to paint; it was so well done it was lifelike. Chris was moved to tears when he saw it; now that they were gone, he missed them more than ever.

"I need to return to London soon," he said to me after breakfast early one morning while we lingered over coffee in the dining room. Our guests had departed and the house was now relatively quiet.

"I know," I sighed softly. "How long do you expect to be gone?"

"Not long, actually. Most of the paper work is finished; Wesley has made arrangements to have the furniture Chloe wanted shipped to her in Los Angeles. My parents left the preponderance of their estate to her, at my request. My father set aside most of his personal items for me or Scott, and they also bequeathed something for each of your children and grandchildren to remember them by."

"That was sweet of them," I said, feeling the loss of my in-laws as keenly as their son.

"Dad was a rock and Mum was a sweetheart!" Christopher said with a profound look of pleasure. "They were wonderful people, Rachel!"

"I know, Darling," I said, taking his hand in mine.

"They were good people, too, gentlepeople whom I truly admired."

"Yes, they were both gentle and strong," I said in agreement.

"They didn't have easy childhoods; they weren't privileged by any means. Mum had it a bit harder than Dad though," he said in reflection. "I don't know if she ever told you that she was raised by her stepmother."

"No, she didn't," I replied in answer.

"Her mother died when she was only two years old; it was difficult for her father to care for her and work so he left her with his parents until he remarried when she was about five years old."

"That must have been difficult for her," I said.

"I don't know…perhaps. Mum never said really. She loved her stepmother very much even though she thought she was somewhat rigid; she knew she was a good woman and she was grateful to her for all she did."

"I think people faced life more realistically then, don't you?" I asked seriously. "Like Papa and Grandmother, they always seemed to accept the fact that life would present them with problems they would need to cope with and they did; they didn't think of themselves as victims or look for someone to blame or for a way of escape."

"Mother had a wonderful attitude about life," he said, "and loved to tell me stories of her childhood, which was relatively happy in spite of their poverty. She said she realized when she married and began raising her own family that she had learned a great deal about contentment from her stepmother. She said that what they lacked never really mattered because they found joy just being with one another."

Just then Patricia came to the dining room door and informed Chris he had a telephone call; he left to answer it while I finished my coffee. When he returned a short time later, we finished discussing his travel plans.

"I may have to make a brief trip to Madrid after I finish in London," he said woefully. "James said he's considering filming a small portion of our new movie there; the location scout found a perfect spot but I probably need to look at it myself to be sure."

"How long do you think you'll be gone this time?" I questioned, trying not to sound too disappointed.

"I'm hoping it won't take more than two weeks to finish the estate business and then I'll probably jet over to Spain for a few days. Oh, by the way, Mother left a gift for you, too."

"A gift for me?" I said surprised.

"Yes, and I'm not allowed to tell you what it is. I was going to bring it back with me but I left in such a hurry I forgot; I'll have Wesley send it home."

"What is it?" I asked inquisitively.

"It's a surprise, so I can't tell," he said with a light laugh.

"Oh, come on, Chris, you're not going to make me wait?" I whined out loud with a smile.

"Patience is a virtue, Darling!" he replied with a graceful grin.

Chapter Five

Honoring Life

Christopher was on his way to London by the following weekend; Wesley met him at Heathrow Airport and together they drove to the flat Chris still maintained in the city. Handling his parents' estate had been a difficult task because it meant truly saying good-bye. Death had brought a permanent end to their temporal lives and the beginning of their eternal ones; therefore, their deaths brought both grief and joy.

Morgan and Clare Elliott had been honorable parents; Chris revered them as heroes, always treating them with the respect and admiration he felt they deserved. He couldn't understand the general public who lived in awe of sports and movie stars, possibly because he knew so many of them personally who lacked any noble qualities worthy of adulation. No, Chris knew it took courage and tenacity to go to work day after day, sometimes to an unrewarding job struggling to provide for those one loved. These were real heroes deserving of earthly praise but all too few acknowledged it.

My husband had been gone several days when the first of numerous packages began to arrive at the estate. They were of a variety of sizes, weights and shapes and each was addressed to a different member of the family. I had Patrick store all of the boxes in one of the upstairs storage rooms until we could gather everyone together for their unveiling.

Days after all the large boxes arrived, a security courier arrived to hand-deliver a special package that required my personal signature. Christopher had called to tell me it was coming and that I had permission to open it upon its arrival; I couldn't wait.

The box was larger than I expected and once the courier had gone, I carried it into the parlor and set it down on the coffee table in front of my favorite chair. Upon opening the package I was surprised to find yet another box inside; it was smaller and made from mahogany, a wood my grandfather always loved. The box had the figure of a Victorian woman carved in the top; it was remarkably ornate and the craftsmanship was exquisite. When I opened the lid I was surprised to find a purple velvet jewel box enclosed inside; it was soft and luxurious. On top of the jewel box was an envelope with my name scrawled on the outside. Leaving the jewel box in its place, I removed the envelope, and retrieved the sheets of stationery it held. Quietly, I settled back into my chair to read the epistle, which had been written by Clare.

> *My Dearest Rachel,*
>
> *Our days are passing quickly; Morgan and I will not long remain a part of this world but we eagerly await our eternal reward and are prepared to enter the pearly gates, to walk upon heaven's streets of gold and, to finally meet the divine Lord, in person, face to face. What a wonderful day that will be!*
>
> *This delightful box was a very special gift to me from my faithful husband on my fiftieth birthday; the jewels came ten years later. It is my heartfelt desire to bequeath them to you; I pray that they will be a fond remembrance of us and the love we have felt for you.*
>
> *Rachel, you are a lily among thorns; a truly virtuous woman. Life hasn't been easy for you, I know; it can be so complicated at times. But you have triumphed over adversity and grown wise as a result; and your sagacious counsel is the real beauty of your character.*

In marrying our son, Christopher, you stepped into the difficult position of being a second wife and a stepmother, which very often poses unique relational problems for new families. And yet because of your humility you handled both stations with grace and charm. You have been a truly wonderful daughter in so many ways and we thank you profoundly. God bless you my dear, God bless you always.

All my love,
Clare

I folded the letter and placed it back into the envelope; my tear-filled eyes found it difficult to focus. I used a tissue to dry them and after removing the purple jewel box from its container, I opened the lid. Nestled inside was a necklace and matching earrings of oval shaped sapphires encircled with diamonds. I was in awe!

Clare Elliott had been a very genteel woman; Chloe was like her in many ways. They were both blessed with the same lovely eyes and winsome smile and when they spoke, the same soft melodious tones came forth.

I put down the lid of the jewel case and leaned back into my chair, closing my eyes to the world. It was in this room so many years before that this lovely gray-haired woman had shared so much of herself with me, my family and friends.

She was so delicate when she spoke of being newly married; how terrified she felt to be a new bride. The silver candlesticks she and Morgan had received as a wedding gift from her mother and dad were now seated upon our mantle; she said that we should keep them and then pass them on to Chloe. I opened my eyes and glanced over at the fireplace mantle where they were situated; they were decades old but they were still bright and shiny, symbols of their lifelong commitment to each other.

Chris called that evening and I told him how pleased I was to receive his mother's gift. We talked about family and the things happening around us before he told me he was flying to Spain and then would return home.

Finally, on a wet weekend in March, when we were all together again, the family gathered in the parlor to open their gifts from Morgan and Clare.

Victoria and Allen received a collection of rare books; Devon inherited an artist's rendering of a mother and child at the seashore, while Charlotte and Edgar acquired a portion of their record collection; even Martha and Mary were blessed with a gift of exquisite ceramic bowls and cookbooks to share. All of our grandchildren received gifts as well: books, toys or artwork.

Chloe and Scott had inherited the lion's share of their estate, which totaled more than one million pounds. It was hard to believe his working-class parents had amassed such a fortune. Furniture and personal items that she chose to keep had been shipped to their home and would arrive over time. My in-laws had even set up a separate trust fund for baby Caitlin, which she would receive when she turned twenty-five.

Christopher was touched by the generosity of his parents; he frequently spoke of the values they taught him when he was young, which he adhered to as a man. He said they helped him form the moral compass he still lived by.

Over dinner on Sunday night, Chris eagerly shared stories of his childhood, and explained how his parents had acquired their small fortune. He seemed especially pleased that they had bestowed their family heirlooms upon all the members of our family; they would forever be gentle reminders of those who had gone before us and touched our hearts while they were here.

"Chloe," Chris said while motioning to his daughter once dinner was over, "I need to speak with you privately for a moment."

Chloe gave Caitlin to her father and then left the room with Chris; when they rejoined the group for dessert in the parlor a little while later it was obvious she had been crying.

"Is everything okay?" I asked her, concerned. Chloe put her arms around my waist and gave me a huge hug.

"Everything's fine, Mom," she replied, and handed me an envelope. "Open it!" she said and I complied. Inside was a letter; I could tell it was from Clare. The same stationery and handwriting that penned my epistle had penned this one. "Read it!" she said taking a cup of tea from the tea cart. She made herself comfortable on the sofa by the fire near her husband and daughter, who was sleeping sounding in her father's arms.

I opened up the letter, sat down in my chair and began to read Chloe's letter.

Dearest Chloe,

Grandfather and I are nearing the end of our lives; we know that you will grieve for us when we are gone. But death is not the end, my dear, for we will all meet again one day in the holy city above.

You have blessed our lives, Chloe; you have become the woman we prayed for; and the woman your mother longed to see. Her early demise was unfortunate, but a fragrant reminder of her delightful life was left behind in you.

Chloe, life is full of mystery; savor every moment. Enjoy your lovely little family as the generous gift from God they are. Treat your husband with respect; he loves you dearly. Train your daughter to revere God, to honor her parents and to respect herself. Keep her close while she is young, but don't be afraid to set her free when her time for independence arrives. Remember, she is on loan to you temporarily, as her life belongs to her Lord.

I wish I could remember my own dear mother; I've always regretted having no memory of her. But God blessed me with a second mother who grew to love me like one of her own. She was the only mother I ever really knew; she is the one who taught me about life and through her example I learned the importance of truth and honesty and self-respect. She taught me to think for myself, to behave modestly and to love unconditionally and with generosity.

Chloe, God gives and he takes away. Your own dear mother has passed on to glory but another good mother has come into your life, not to take her place, but rather to assist you in areas she no longer can. She's an extraordinary woman and, a faithful friend; don't ever be afraid to embrace her completely. She is God's gift to you; love and honor her as you did your own dear mother.

Well, my dear, it is time to say good-bye to you. Our lives may be over but our memory will live on in you and in your children.

All my love,
Grandmother Clare

⌒ Chapter Six ⌒

Rights and Privileges

Chloe was deeply touched by her grandmother's endearing letter; I was as well. It was a keepsake to be cherished throughout her lifetime just as I treasured the writings my own dear mother had left behind. They were, in essence, a part of the person that we had known and loved, a memory to be shared with future generations.

I was pleasantly thrilled that the children had agreed to make the weekend a long one, arranging to stay over an extra day. We had a delightful evening in the parlor and while the family ate the delectable desserts Martha and Mary had prepared, Charlotte and Edgar entertained us with an assortment of musical selections.

"This ginger-spice cake Martha baked is delicious," Victoria said, devouring her last mouthful.

"I thought the chocolate mousse was heavenly," Devon replied.

"I know the children loved their cupcakes," Charlotte said, taking a break from the piano.

"That's because Martha always fills them with colored whipped cream," I said with a hearty laugh.

"Caitlin certainly enjoyed hers," Chloe said, "although I think she's wearing a good portion of it. I'll have to give her a bath and wash the green frosting out of her red hair," she giggled.

"Caty's beginning to look a lot like you, Chloe," I said thoughtfully, "except for her hair."

"I love the red color," Chloe beamed proudly. "It goes beautifully with her green eyes. She inherited those genes from Scott's biological mother; his hair is more auburn and it's nice that his adoptive father has red hair as well."

"Do you see your biological parents much, Scott?" Edgar asked, eating a hearty piece of spice cake generously covered with caramel sauce.

"No, I don't see them very often," he said meditatively. "Chloe met my mother after we got married and then again after Caitlin was born; I haven't seen my biological father in some time. They were only sixteen when I was conceived; they didn't want to get married and their families jointly agreed that adoption was their best option. They wanted to go on with their individual lives and, fortunately, they didn't believe in abortion," Scott said, relating a part of his history with the family.

"My adoptive parents lived in a neighboring town; they were friends of close friends of my parent's family who knew about the pregnancy and facilitated the adoption. After I was born my adoptive parents allowed my biological parents to visit me when they wanted to, and when I grew older they provided me with access to them if and when I wanted it. I saw them infrequently until I was a teenager; at that time I came to realize they had other lives that really didn't include me and I elected to see them less and less.

"I feel fortunate that I had great adoptive parents who I really regard as my real parents; they raised me as their own and treated me with love and kindness. My dad was a great guy and a hard worker; he was stern when he needed to be but he was respectful and honest. Mom was the epitome of grace; but when justice needed to be served, Mom served it with love. I couldn't have asked for better role models although there were times I didn't appreciate them or respect them. Today, I know how blessed I was that God called two perfectly wonderful strangers to embrace me and give me a home; more importantly, they shared their faith and it became the anchor of my soul."

"Wow," Edgar replied, "I've never heard anyone speak so eloquently about their parents, Scott."

"Perhaps that's because I've had a lot of years to ponder the rights and privileges I acquired as a son that came not by birth but rather by selection. And I use the word *selection* carefully because I truly believe God placed me into my adoptive family; I really don't believe in chance, or coincidence like some," he said, sipping his coffee. Scott was a very analytical man and it was obvious he had given a great deal of thought to the subject that became the evening's topic of discussion.

"Adoption begins as a legal transaction," he began thoughtfully, "and in the process new parents gift their chosen child with the status and privileges of a biological child. Invariably, that gift requires the cooperation of both parties to be fully enjoyed. And, when the adoptive child grows to maturity, he or she must realize that their adoption obligates them to assume and perform all the duties of a legitimate child. Personally, I don't take those responsibilities lightly and I no longer consider them simply 'duties' just as my adoptive parents don't consider me the product of a 'legal transaction' because we love each other.

"I didn't always feel this way; I've arrived at this stage of reasoning over time mostly because I'm grateful for the family that received me as their own, and guided me through life teaching me by their example a healthy respect for God and mankind."

"The Romans often adopted a beloved slave as a son," Allen began, "and the ceremony…" he went on to give the customs and laws of their culture and spoke a little about those of the Greeks. I listened quietly, still reflecting on Scott's declaration of love for his parents; it was tender and insightful but more than that it allowed us a more intimate glimpse into the heart of the man. Hearing Scott speak helped me appreciate more fully why Christopher had asked him to be on the board of trustees for Noah's Ark. The ministry had been established as a haven of rest for lost teens and abused animals; we hoped the inhabitants would find healing and a new beginning, which eventually would lead to adoption.

Noah's Ark was prospering under its exemplary resident managers, Pastor Eli Samuels and his wife, Susanna. They were a multi-ethnic couple who were also retired licensed clinicians. The ranch they lived at and worked on was located to the south of our estate; we had purchased it a few years earlier specifically for this purpose.

The main house, built in the shape of a horseshoe, sat on a small incline above the highway across from the ocean. It was surrounded by a multitude of tall trees, which kept it cool during the warm summer weather.

Out back, some distance to the rear of the house, was a horse stable of substantial proportions; it housed the good work horses we inherited with the property. Christopher, an outstanding equestrian, had purchased several additional riding horses so he could indulge in one of his favorite pastimes when at home.

The ranch property extended far into the hills where the cattle roamed freely; several barns were located in various areas on the outer perimeter along with staff housing; some of these units had been converted into residential living quarters for our conflicted teens and their chaperons.

When renovation of the ranch began, Chris had several of his set-director friends design and then build a small country town reminiscent of the early 1900s; these buildings were all created to function in a variety of ways. The old-time general store was currently being used to teach multiple classes from ethics to economics. The saloon built nearby functioned as a mess hall and served only non-alcoholic beverages while providing a large open stage for talented performers engaged in the study of the arts. The small town hall built across from the general store was the seat of government whereby our small community of residents was educated in history and political science. And the most recent addition to the campus was an old country church where biblical messages were preached and a variety of languages were taught. All of our educators were either members of the staff or local teachers living in the community who came to the campus every weekday.

Besides attending classes all our teenage residents participated in learning the business of cattle ranching. They were up early each morning, worked long days and retired early most evenings. Life on the ranch wasn't a picnic, but those who came to Noah's Ark were there by choice. Most had few other options and all were in desperate need of a new beginning.

The residents of the ranch were a mixture of adolescents that had become wards of the court for a variety of reasons; some were abused, some in trouble with the law, some simply neglected. All were in need of love, structure and hope.

"Rachel," Chris called, regaining my attention, "would you like more tea?"

"No, thank you." I replied with a smile and when Charlotte returned to the piano I requested she play an old favorite.

Chapter Seven

To and Fro

Spending time with Myra Clayborn was an advantage I looked forward to; her cast had finally been removed and she was now in the process of undergoing physical therapy to regain the graceful use of her mended broken leg. Confinement had been a difficult challenge for her, even though she managed to use her captive time wisely. And when we spoke I sensed her eagerness to pursue the tasks that had been suspended during her convalescence, and yet wisdom kept her from rushing ahead. "We should take the time to pray about our misadventures," she said while we conversed on the telephone. "God sometimes chooses unusual ways to redirect us," she laughed, "and often when we least expect it."

I drove down south in June to spend a week visiting family and friends, while Christopher was off again surveying possible locations for his latest movie. I chose to stay at Charlotte's home, which was convenient, comfortable and secure as well as being situated in close proximity to almost everyone I wanted to see.

On the day I drove into Ventura to visit with Myra, the weather was cool and the air was rather brisk; the blue sky was dotted with a smattering of white billowy clouds that reminded me of large fluffy pillows. The ocean waves calmly beat upon the sandy brown shore that lay west of the freeway, and with the sun roof open the noisy gulls flying overhead could be heard bantering back and forth, apparently looking for a morning morsel of food.

Sam drove the black sedan I traveled in while Prudence rode in the back with me. My two personal bodyguards who accompanied me everywhere I went were silent spectators to the more personal aspects of my life. I had grown so accustomed to their perpetual presence that being alone sometimes felt unnatural; it was almost eerie.

We exited the highway and headed east into the foothills, which were a beautiful shade of green thanks to the abundant rain, toward Myra's home. Driving up into the hills we passed the First National Bank Building, located at 21 South California Street. The stately edifice was four stories tall and included elements of the Renaissance revival-style architecture; it housed the second law office of Erle Stanley Gardner, the creator of Perry Mason, one of my favorite characters. Just around the corner at 16 North Oak Street, stood the two-story Bank of Ventura Building; it housed the first Ventura law office Mr. Gardner inhabited while a practicing attorney. They were located in close proximity to the Ventura City Hall, formerly the Ventura County Courthouse; it was fascinating to see the sights that must have inspired the author to create his stories about the world famous attorney while he practiced law in California in the early part of the 1900s.

Myra's picturesque home was situated at the top of a hill; her Queen Anne style residence was only one in a city where there were many beautiful homes of this style architecture. Built sometime in the 1890s it was painted a lovely shade of pale yellow; it had a wrap-around porch on the first story and a large balcony porch on the second story, which permitted a breath-taking view of the Pacific Ocean, gleaming brightly today beneath the warm rays of the sun. Her lovely garden was resplendent with a variety of colorful flowers, lush greenery and tall palm trees swaying gently in the breeze. A long row of plum trees lined the back wall of her yard, covered with a bountiful harvest.

"Your gardens are lovely," I said to Myra while enjoying a leisurely brunch of crumpets and jam on her backyard patio.

"Thank you, they're lovely all year long but more so when the flowers are in bloom," she sighed in agreement. "And this plum jam was made by one of my daughters," she added holding a small ivory jam pot in her hands.

"It's delicious," I replied, taking another bite of the sweet preserves covering my whole-wheat crumpet.

"If you like, I'll send you a few baskets of fruit," she generously offered. "My trees produce abundantly every year."

"Oh, that would be lovely," I said thanking her. "Martha takes time once a week to teach a cooking class at Noah's Ark. I believe she's going to include a class on preserving this autumn; it's an art few people indulge in anymore."

"Ah, yes," she said shaking her head and sipping a cup of tea. "Women are much too interested in other pursuits; these 'old-fashioned' arts seem to be silently slipping away from us."

"It's sad, isn't it?" I asked pensively.

"Yes, it is," Myra said with a wistful smile, "in more ways than we currently know, I'm afraid. Domestic life can be extremely rewarding but it isn't glamorous; and besides being routine and mundane it can also be hard work. The dividends don't accumulate quickly either," she continued, "because they are produced over a lifetime.

"We're fortunate that we women have had the doors of education opened to us; we have so many more career opportunities now than we did decades ago. And yet, I can't help but think that in many ways we've been tempted to pursue a path that isn't entirely beneficial." Myra continued to sip her tea slowly while I digested her observations.

"I think…in a way…that we're being deceived, Rachel. We're being programmed to think we can have it all, and that's impossible. A successful career comes at a price; it isn't free and I think it often ends up costing us much more than we're willing to pay. Something is usually sacrificed on its altar: a marriage, children, ethics, morality, perhaps even sanity."

Myra's thoughts were heavy; they made me stop and think about my own life. There were times I resented the fact that I had given up my college education to marry Paul and then have children. But now that so many women were being forced into the labor force due to economics, I realized that I had been very fortunate to remain at home and raise my girls. Besides which being wealthy enough to have maids allowed me a great deal of freedom to devote to my outside interests.

"Don't you believe that a woman's education is a practical necessity today?" I asked after reflecting on her comments. "Or at the very least that she needs to be trained vocationally to be able to support herself and her family?"

"I do, Rachel. I agree with both of those statements. I do however also believe that it's extremely important for women, mothers really, to be at home nurturing their children as they grow and mature. And yet, I also understand how difficult and costly that can be. Those who must work to survive have a heavy load cast upon their shoulders. Working and raising a family is an arduous task; everyone loses when mothers have to enter the labor force."

"But they aren't the ones you're thinking of, are they?" I asked intuitively.

"No, they aren't. I'm thinking of the women who work because they want."

"They want?" I inquired.

"Yes, they want…they desire…they lust. The attractions today are the same as they've always been; women are no different than men; they too lust for physical reasons, for emotional reasons and for intellectual reasons. We want satisfying relationships, aesthetic pleasures and fame and adulation.

"Many people search for these things because of an inner emptiness; inwardly they're unfulfilled and dissatisfied with their lives so they seek to find the things they *think* will make them happy.

"Those who seek satisfaction through love often move from one sexual relationship to another, which leads to isolation. Those who seek satisfaction through pleasure often seek to acquire possessions, which leads to desolation. Those who seek satisfaction through fame often pursue careers sacrificing all on the altar of success, which leads to despair."

Myra smiled at me; I sensed she realized how lost I was in her analogy.

"You don't understand, do you?" she asked kindly.

"No, not entirely I'm afraid."

"People desire something to fill up the empty hole within, either consciously or unconsciously. That hole however can only be filled by that which it was created to hold. People were created to be in relationship with God Almighty and have his essence dwelling within. People may try to fill that space with a variety of things, but things will only leave them feeling dissatisfied. Sin separates us from the one relationship that will bring eternal happiness; sin separates us from God and isolation results. Possessions decay; they remind us that we are mortal and desolation results. Fame is fleeting; it has no eternal value and leaves us barren and forsaken, and despair results.

"Love, material possessions and fame are not evil; but good becomes evil when it deceives or denies us of the best available, and the best available is Jesus Christ. He alone can gratify the desires of every living soul.

"There are billions of empty people in the world seeking satisfaction; they are on a quest, traveling to and fro, looking for answers that will satisfy their voracious appetites. And they end up wandering aimlessly because the answers they seek can only be found in God."

I pondered Myra's words without comment. The wind picked up and whistled through the trees and my attention was diverted by an airplane flying noiselessly overhead. It made me think about modern transportation, which made it possible for globetrotters and jet-setters to travel around the world in relative ease. What were they looking for? I asked myself, and my mind opened a little to what Myra was saying.

"What you're actually saying is that people aren't content, and the reason they aren't content is because they're in pain, is that right? They want to find a remedy for their pain so they look for it in distant places, or in foreign cultures, and sometimes even in experiencing new religions. Is that what you're saying?"

"Yes, Rachel," she said placing her tea cup on the table. "I'm sorry; I didn't mean to allow our conversation to grow so heavy. It's just that these are the things that I think about and I believe you're someone who can understand my concerns. People, either consciously or unconsciously, are looking for solutions to whatever causes them pain. They want to fill up the void in order to stop the throbbing of their hearts; and when the throbbing becomes unbearable they turn to a number of things: sex, drugs, alcohol, whatever anesthetizes their pain even if only momentarily.

"And this is what concerns me because eventually, someone is going to come along and offer the hurting inhabitants of the world a solution to all that ails them; he will promise them lasting peace and an end to their pain!"

"But only God can do that!" I stated rather emphatically.

"Yes, that's true. Unfortunately, people don't want the peace that God offers through a humble carpenter from Nazareth. They're looking for someone bigger and brighter…someone more magnanimous…a charismatic leader they can worship and adore. And he's coming, Rachel. I sense his presence already. He will be a beast at heart and the false peace he will bring shall destroy many."

~ *Chapter Eight* ~

Renewal

*T*he wind changed dramatically as the morning passed and when the air grew chilly we strolled indoors to continue our conversation. Myra escorted me to her library and study; it was a charming room painted in creamy yellow; one entire wall, from floor to ceiling, was covered with shelves of books. A set of forest green leather chairs surrounded a round oak study table in one corner of the room with a lamp hanging overhead. There was a large fireplace with a carved oak mantle in the middle of one wall; it was decorated with several lovely pots and jars of ancient origins. Directly opposite the fireplace was a comfortable couch covered in slate blue velvet; lamps stood as sentinels at either end while a small oval table sat alone in front, the bearer of a vase of calla lilies and green ferns. A round china cabinet in one corner was filled with knickknacks, and an old dresser in another corner sported an assortment of pictures of family members and friends.

The room was warm and welcoming and the ancient tomes resting upon the bookshelves greeted us like old familiar friends. I glanced over the titles and saw many personal favorites. Myra and I sat on the couch and discussed several of the authors represented in her library and found we had very similar tastes in literature.

The wood floor was decorated with a large tapestry that had a floral design predominantly in bright hues of yellow and blue; the rug was edged in dark green blending all the colors of the room together nicely. A long rectangular window to the rear of the sofa was swathed in floral curtains that matched the pattern in the carpet; streams of soft light filtered through the opaque glass to brighten the room.

The change of atmosphere shifted the focus of our conversation, which went from favorite books and authors to the progress being made on the church school building restoration. The earthquake had significantly damaged the old brick edifice but fortunately it was structurally intact. Renovation had always been a part of the plan to bring it up to current building and safety codes, I told Myra; it would just take longer than originally expected.

The earthquake had taken a large toll on several of the small coastal communities in our area, but we were fortunate to see good things happening as a result in that it brought a measure of needed revitalization to the area. Unfortunately, Grandfather's mansion did suffer some structural damage in the basement, which affected a portion of the secret tunnel that led to a trap door under the chapel. And Patrick and Chris were in the process of resolving the difficulty of restoring the integrity of the building without advertising the existence of the tunnel. I was afraid it wouldn't be easy.

Myra and I went on to share our thoughts on the process of renewal and how wonderful it was to see dead things rise from the grave to new life. It reminded me of the restoration of the Victorian home we had purchased in Petaluma, now a functioning restaurant called Sweet Dreams, which I hoped Myra would one day be able to visit.

In our brief time together we were each able to share more about ourselves in order to get to know one another better; our friendship was growing.

"I so desperately wanted to live a full and fascinating life when I was young," Myra began with a wry smile, "just like many others I suppose, that I did a great many foolish things—things I ultimately regretted later on. Fortunately, the Good Shepherd is very patient with his foolish sheep, especially those who end up wounded and bleeding." Myra looked directly into my eyes. "You were wounded and bleeding too, weren't you, Rachel?" she asked.

"I was," I replied in a whisper, feeling my throat tighten with emotion.

"I'm so sorry," she replied understandingly. Myra then rose from the sofa and excused herself for a moment and quietly disappeared from sight.

I closed my eyes, suppressing the tears that came from within. Regardless of the pain I experienced, I had survived. I took a tissue from my purse to wipe my eyes, and looking out the open window, my eyes rested on the flowers in bloom. And then I realized that I hadn't just survived my divorce, because the life I once shared with Paul died and a new one with Christopher took its place. I had been reborn just like the seed that's sown into the ground, which dies before it brings forth new life.

In our agricultural community the laws of sowing and reaping were on constant display; the business of cultivating the soil, producing crops and raising livestock was marked by the changing seasons. Farming was a business, a science, an art and a way of life for many of my friends and neighbors.

The process of 'keeping the land' was as old as the creation, when man was divinely given the ability to care for and nurture the earth from which he had been formed. Dominion was once ours, I thought to myself; but we lost it because of disobedience.

"Cursed is the ground," God said to Adam. And now, thorns and thistles reign everywhere man does not strive to "keep" the land.

When Myra returned, she was carrying a small earthenware planter filled with a beautiful African violet.

"This is for you, Rachel," she said placing the vessel on the table in front of me.

"Why, it's lovely, Myra," I said gratefully. "Thank you! I love this luxurious deep purple color, and the leaves are just like velvet."

"They're one of my favorites; I have several varieties growing in my kitchen window and thought this one would suit you," she replied with a generous smile.

"The earth produces such abundant beauty when we respect it."

"It does indeed," she admitted. "I'm only sorry we haven't been better landowners," she quietly added. "Instead, we behave like tyrants and bullies; people don't realize that even the land has rights," Myra interjected. "Actions have consequences, and men continue to incur a heavy debt due to their handling of the environment; payment is about to be exacted."

"You can see what's coming, can't you?" I asked softly.

"Famine, disease, pestilence; I'm afraid they're already here, Rachel; they are the harbingers of doom. As the clock continues to tick, these woes will become more frequent and intense as the earth calls to God for its redemption."

"Just as we mortals await our final emancipation from the body," I said, returning to my thoughts of new life, which proceeds only from death.

"If only men could see!"

~ *Chapter Nine* ~

Hebrew Lessons

*T*he day spent with Myra had been enlightening but disquieting; her views of the future were wrapped around the prophecies currently being fulfilled through a multitude of global catastrophes. Her beliefs were organized, succinct and, in my opinion, extremely on course. "The beginning of the end has begun," she said, unequivocally. "The innocent will suffer along with the guilty, just as the sun shines on the good and the evil."

Myra told me she openly shares her heart with people, not to instill fear but rather to inspire action before it is too late. A little introspection would do us all a great deal of good, I thought, on my drive back to Charlotte's. We who believed the world would one day end had a responsibility to educate those who scoffed at the message. The task was daunting but not impossible. We simply had to "go, and make disciples!"

Charlotte's children greeted me with open arms when I arrived at their home. E.J. was proud of the fact that he had finally grown taller than his older twin sister Eliza, even if it was only by a quarter of an inch. Ethan, I thought, would eventually surpass them both. He was a much bigger child even if he was a few years younger. All three children looked a great deal alike; they had sandy blonde curly hair and green eyes. Ethan had a rounder face, more cherubic than either of his siblings, and was beginning to resemble his father's father a great deal.

On Saturday morning we all drove down to Devon's home located just off Sunset Boulevard in an old but quiet neighborhood; Chloe and Caitlin had planned to meet us as well for a small family reunion and a trip to the Getty Museum.

"Mom," Devon waved from the front porch as we approached the house, "it's so good to see you." My middle daughter was beaming with joy; she was a woman of immense fortitude and it gave me great pleasure to see her so happy. Joseph's tragic death had been difficult for her but she had managed to rise above her own grief to make a warm and secure home for Devorah, her only daughter.

Devorah, whom we had called Dari almost since birth, had grown up too; Devorah Anne Rabinowitz was an intelligent child, almost a prodigy. Intellectually, she was a great deal like her parents: a whiz at science and math. Physically, she had Devon's fair skin tone, blonde hair and blue eyes but she had her father's tall, thin frame. Spiritually, she was extremely sensitive and very discerning.

Mary, Martha's sister and Devon's housekeeper, had a delicious morning snack waiting for us when we arrived; both sisters excelled in the kitchen! An assortment of fresh fruit—strawberries, grapes and melon balls—were mixed in small bowls for each of us. She also baked big, gooey chocolate chip cookies and formed them like small saucers; these we could enjoy when we returned home later that afternoon.

Chloe arrived shortly after us, greeting each of her stepsisters with a hug and kiss. Caitlin Rose was still a little shy but always enthused to be visiting her older cousins. Her red hair was long but thin and Chloe kept it braided tightly on play days; her green eyes almost always shined with wonder.

We enjoyed our snack and then packed up the cars to drive to the museum, only a few miles away. The children had been to the museum often with their parents usually on Saturdays when the Getty conducted what was called an "Artful Weekend." Children could enjoy an outdoor workshop designed to exercise their imagination by allowing them to create their own masterpieces, something my grandchildren loved to do.

Today, we planned to visit two of the exhibits: *Rembrandt's Late Religious Portraits* in the Exhibitions Pavilion and *The Making of Furniture* housed in the South Pavilion on the Plaza Level.

I was excited about seeing each display but I was keenly interested in viewing firsthand the French marquetry table they had on display in three stages of completion. Contemporary craftsman had collaborated to showcase the craftsmanship involved in the production of a table made in the mid-eighteenth century; it proved to be fascinating. My interest was enhanced essentially due to the fact that my own ancestors had hailed from France and my grandfather had been a carpenter. His small furniture business had flourished and grown into a tiny empire, which over a period of time consisted not only of his own regal line of household furnishings but later was expanded to include a large import and export business dealing in a variety of costly European antiques.

As a child, I watched him with awe as he worked at his craft, and fortunately I still owned many of the original pieces he designed. Grandfather was a creative and enterprising young man who, after bringing his family to the United States to live, opened his first furniture store and import-export business in Brooklyn, New York. His diligence and industry coupled with integrity brought him amazing success, which enabled him to amass the fortune I had acquired as his only living descendant.

The children were eager to view the religious portraits Rembrandt van Rijn, a Dutch painter of the seventeenth century, had painted as they included images of religious figures they could identify from Scripture.

There wouldn't be time today to visit the *Photographs of Paul Strand* exhibition or the *Oil Sketches by Giovanni Battista Tiepolo*, an Italian artist; we would have to see them another day.

The children's workshop was held at 11 A.M. in the Family Room Patio; we then went to the South Pavilion for the furniture exhibition before stopping for lunch at the Garden Terrace. Our final stop was the Rembrandt exhibition, which was quite popular today judging by the numbers of visitors attending the presentation.

Those viewing the portraits were visibly moved by the beauty of each work on display; a family standing nearby appeared to be discussing one of the portraits of Christ. I realized when we drew closer that they were all speaking Hebrew, a fact which did not go unnoticed by my young granddaughter Dari, who was holding my hand.

"Shalom!" she said casually to a young girl standing just outside her family's small circle. The youngster smiled and said, "Shalom!" and the girls entered into a brief conversation. Her name, Dari told me while making introductions, was Leah; she and her family were on vacation and visiting from Israel. They had family that lived in the Fairfax District of Los Angeles and this was their first trip to the United States.

Devon, who had been talking to Charlotte several feet away, walked across the room to join Dari, whom Leah was now introducing to her family. Devon, in English, introduced herself to Leah's parents; they told her they were pleasantly surprised to find a young American girl conversant in the Hebrew language. Devon then explained that Dari's father had been Jewish; it was he who began her Hebrew education when she was only a baby. After Joseph died, Devon continued Dari's Hebrew lessons with a friend who was also a Hebrew scholar; they met regularly twice a week.

When we were on our way home that afternoon, Devon asked Dari what had inspired her to speak to the young Israeli girl.

"They were discussing the portraits of Yeshua," she responded casually, "and my heart broke for them. You see, they spoke of what a great prophet he was but didn't believe that he was the promised Messiah spoken of in the Scriptures. I wanted to tell them they were wrong, but I wasn't sure that I could. So, instead, I simply said hello. One day, when I'm ready, perhaps I'll be able to tell them. Leah gave me her address so we can write to each other and eventually I'll see her again, when I go to Israel."

"When you go to Israel?" Devon questioned lightheartedly.

"Yes," Dari replied casually. "My future lies there with my father's people."

Devon looked at her daughter with concern. "What do you mean, Dari? Your future is here, in America, with your family."

"No, Mother," she replied with stern determination. "My future lies in Israel with the people of my father. I am going to be a fisher of men; I want to be able to tell them of Yeshua and how he came to die for their sins."

Chapter Ten

Queen Bee

*D*evon was visibly surprised by Dari's intense profession but said nothing further. Mary was busy preparing dinner for us when we arrived home energized by the day's activities; we were all extremely hungry and the children quickly gobbled down a cookie and then ran to Dari's room to play until called for dinner.

The girls and I set the dining room table for the adults; the children set the patio table for them to eat at as there wasn't enough room in Devon's small home for everyone to sit down together. Mary prepared a delectable feast of home-fried chicken, potato salad, string beans, corn on the cob, fresh watermelon and hot buttermilk biscuits; it was amazing that we still had room for dessert but no one passed up Mary's fresh blueberry cobbler.

Charlotte, who had driven her own car to her sister's home, left with her children after dessert; Chloe, who lived close by, stayed to enjoy a second cup of coffee. Scott was out of town so she longed for a little adult companionship.

Dari and Caitlin watched a video in the small family room while we ladies washed dishes and cleaned up the kitchen. An hour later Chloe departed with Caitlin for home; Dari went to bed and Devon and I sat on the couch talking.

"Mother, I'm really concerned about Dari," she began softly. "I think she completely misunderstood her father's purpose in giving her that fishing pole before he died. I'm positive he never meant to give her the idea he wanted her to be an evangelist!"

"Perhaps he didn't, Devon, but that's something she will probably come to realize when she gets older. Do you think she's being harmed in any way now by pursuing what she believes may have been his dream for her?" I asked objectively.

"No. I'm only concerned about her focus; I don't want to see her direct all her energy and attention toward this one goal; you know how stubborn she can be."

"Yes, I wonder where she gets it from," I laughed.

"Mother, please, be serious!" Devon cried. "Dari is a very gifted child; she has tremendous potential and it's my responsibility to guide her."

"But you are already doing that, Devon. You provide her with an excellent education; you have given her numerous opportunities to learn and study a variety of subjects. She is experiencing life; she seems very well adjusted to me. She is extremely intelligent, more so than any of her peers, I would say. But what else could you be doing that you are not already doing to help her find out where she excels and what she likes?"

"You're right, I know that. I just don't want to see her talent wasted; she has a brilliant mind for math and science and she enjoys those subjects immensely. Don't you see that Dari has the potential to be one of the greatest scientists of our time? Joseph would have been had he lived, and I know how much his research meant to him. It's what we devoted our lives to—searching for ways to cure the pain and suffering of millions of people."

"That may be true, Devon, but Joseph would never have directed Dari toward one particular vocation; he would have given her the same opportunities that you are, and allowed her to make her own decision about her future."

"Yes, I know that. My concern, however, stems from the fact that since he died she seems bent on pursuing the course of action *she believes* he wanted for her and I can't seem to convince her otherwise."

"Then the best thing for you to do is to continue to allow her to experience a variety of things, to guide her as best you can and to pray for God to lead her in the direction he thinks best. Allow for the fact that Joseph's death may have been the catalyst God allowed to send Dari down a different path than either of you would have chosen for her.

"I know you don't want to see her mind wasted; you believe she could be a tremendous benefit to mankind and you may be right. But you seem to have forgotten one key thing."

Devon looked at me with questioning eyes. "I have?" she asked.

"Yes, you have, Devon. You seem to think it is better to save men's bodies than to save men's souls. But remember, we are made from dust and to dust we will return. Only the spirit of man continues on; what benefit is there if you heal a man's body only for him to lose his soul eternally? You want Dari to choose the best path in life; perhaps she already has!"

Devon had asked me to spend the night, which was always difficult because of my bodyguards, as arrangements had to be made to accommodate them as well. I slept in Dari's room where there were two twin beds; Sam and Prudence would stay in the family room taking turns sleeping on a cot.

The next morning I awoke to the heavenly fragrance of hot coffee brewing in the kitchen. I put on my robe and headed in that direction; Mary was busy frying thick slices of country bacon and preparing Belgium waffles with spicy peaches and whipped cream.

"Did you sleep well, Grandma?" Dari asked me at the breakfast table.

"Yes, I did, thank you, Dari," I replied. "Did you?"

"Yes, I always do, thank you."

"Your room is so lovely; it must give you pleasant dreams," I added.

"The palm trees Daddy had painted on the walls look like they really move, don't they, Grandma?"

"Yes, they do," I agreed.

"And the little bees painted on the walls above the sand dunes are there because of my name. Did you know Devorah means "a bee"?

"Yes, I did know that. You were named for Deborah the

prophetess who was also a judge of Israel; some say she was divinely illuminated. She judged the nation while sitting under a palm tree; I guess that's why your Dad had your room painted with a desert scene." Dari smiled. It was one of the last things Joseph had done for her before he died.

"And did you know that the bee was a symbol of an Egyptian monarch?" I added.

Dari grinned and said, "Then perhaps you should call me Queen Dari!" Together we laughed. How could one so young be so intriguing?

We attended late morning services at Devon's church and when we returned home I prepared to leave. I was sorry to say good-bye to my daughter and her little Queen Bee but I had several other friends to see before returning to my ocean-side abode; and it wouldn't be long before we would all be together again. The girls and their families would all be coming home for a month-long vacation before the Fourth of July celebration; the grandchildren in particular were anxious to attend our town's first Independence Day Parade.

On the return trip to Charlotte's home that afternoon, I called Marie from my cell phone to confirm our luncheon date for the following day. Everything was set!

Chapter Eleven

Bitter Mourning

*T*he telephone rang just as we were finishing dinner that evening and Edgar got up from the table to answer it.

"It's for you, Mom," he said, and added as unemotionally as possible, "it's Mara Elegy!"

I knew immediately why Edgar had been fairly reluctant to mention Mara's name; Charlotte and I had reaped a distasteful tongue-lashing from her during our last encounter, which made me a little apprehensive to speak with her. Charlotte had been extremely angered by her abusive remarks; I felt wounded but extended grace because I knew the source of the pain that had made her act so shamefully.

Mara Elegy had been an old friend and neighbor during the years we lived in Lake Sherwood while I was married to Paul Todd. She had been a warm and loving person then, until her husband disappeared with substantial funds from the International Banking firm where he had worked as an accountant. Mara was left alone to face the scrutiny of his employer and law enforcement officials who, for a time, considered her a possible accomplice in his embezzlement. Faced with the additional humiliation of being abandoned, Mara eventually became embittered.

A few weeks after Mara's husband disappeared, his secretary quit her job and left the country for Brazil, her native homeland. It was then that the pieces of the puzzle began to come together and the reality of what actually transpired became evident: the two had worked together in the conspiracy.

In the end, Mara lost her husband, her home, and her income; she was left with four children to support and the tattered remains of her reputation.

Mara was indeed a victim of injustice. I understood her hurt and endeavored to assist her but she remained reclusive and uncommunicative, not willing to expose herself or her pain to anyone.

Later, after she had reentered the job force, we were able to reconnect and I was pleased when she accepted our invitation to attend a Fourth of July barbecue and political rally being held at our ranch. Charlotte and I had been talking by ourselves that evening when Mara approached us. Her greeting was somewhat cool and during our brief encounter she made several flippant remarks about my divorce and remarriage that were extremely unbecoming.

Charlotte, red-faced and angry, was surprised that I had ignored Mara's offensiveness. But I just couldn't bring myself to do anything that would increase her pain, regardless of how cutting her comments were, because I understood how she felt. And so, I simply extended grace and said nothing.

The events of that evening flashed through my mind as I walked to the study and picked up the telephone extension. I softly said hello.

"Rachel…Rachel," she said twice, haltingly. "Rachel, I'm SO sorry," she began tearfully. "I know words can't possibly convey the profound sense of sorrow I feel in my heart for the way I've treated you; to say "I'm sorry" almost sounds trite but I am."

I didn't know what to say; her tearful repentance was so tender that it hurt my heart to hear her apologize.

"Mara, it's okay," I said tearfully. "I truly understand."

"Oh, Rachel, it's been such a long hard journey for me; my path has been shrouded in darkness for years and then…" she stopped suddenly.

"What?" I asked and then waited for a response.

"Rachel, I know how busy you are and I certainly don't deserve any kindness from you, but I was wondering," she stopped to blow her nose and then continued. "I was wondering if you could find it in your heart to meet me for coffee. There's so much I'd like to say, and to share with you, and I'd like to apologize in person. Would you be able to find some time to join me for a cup of coffee while you're down here visiting with Charlotte? I didn't mean to intrude. I called your home first and Martha told me where you were. I just thought...hoped, maybe we could get together."

"Well, I already have plans for tomorrow," I said, reviewing my schedule quickly in my mind, "but the next day would be fine for me if you're available."

"I'll work around your schedule," she said quickly. "Whatever is convenient."

"Would coffee at Starbuck's near your office be okay? I was going into the city to see my hairdresser and I could meet you afterward."

"Great!" she said enthusiastically. "And Rachel, THANK YOU!"

The table had been cleared and the children were getting ready for bed by the time my telephone conversation with Mara ended. I read to the children and joined them in their bedtime prayers, and saying good night, I turned off the lights and joined Charlotte and Edgar for coffee.

"Mom, what did she say?" Charlotte asked, eager to hear about my conversation which I quickly related. "It's amazing," she confessed later. "I never thought you'd hear from her again, Mom, but you were right. Extending grace wasn't easy but it proved to be the best thing you could do."

"Yes, it was. And it's even possible I've regained a lost friend."

Chapter Twelve

A New Song

Marie Marshall, my best friend, looked beautiful. The hair she lost during chemotherapy had grown in fully even though the sandy brown color was speckled with strands of gray.

We spent the day pleasantly relaxing at her new home. She and Thomas had finally decided to move out of the large house they had shared with their two sons and into something newer but smaller and easier to maintain.

Marie had done a lovely job decorating her domicile and had chosen soft pastel colors and comfortable furniture with gentle fabrics. The living room was bright and spacious; the wallpaper covering the walls sported a floral print of tiny peach and blue flowers nestled in sprigs of green moss. The bare wood floors were covered with a large green rug that brought out the beauty of the dark peach sofa and love seat. Two light blue arm chairs of the same fabric complemented the ensemble and there were several small tables of varying sizes but all of same design in and around the room. A variety of plants and family memorabilia were placed throughout making it homey. In one corner stood the only traditional piece of furniture in the room; it was a lovely china cabinet I had given her as a wedding gift years earlier, something from my grandfather's collection.

We spent a quiet day together; Marie was doing extremely well and it almost seemed impossible to believe that she had ever been sick. Her leukemia had been cured by a successful bone marrow transplant and she was happier than ever simply to be alive.

The next day Sam and Prudence drove me into Los Angeles where I met with Jose, my hairstylist, before joining Mara for coffee. She was already waiting for me when I arrived.

"Decaf, non-fat latte, I hope," she said handing me a cup. She had remembered my favorite drink.

"Thank you, Mara! Yes, it's still my favorite. It's sweet that you remembered after all these years," I said and gave her a hug; she was trembling just a little. The café wasn't too busy so we seated ourselves in two large overstuffed chairs to talk while we sipped our drinks.

"Rachel, I can't thank you enough for coming today," she began slowly. There were tears forming in her eyes as she continued and I sensed the stress our meeting must have caused her. "An apology doesn't seem adequate; I don't believe 'I'm sorry' truly covers the shame I feel for the despicable way I treated you at your ranch and in front of your daughter.

"I wanted to see you in person because I felt I owed you not only an apology but an explanation. I've come a long way in the past year but I had help getting here; Rachel, I'm getting married in the fall. I met a man, we work together, and his name is Everett Lawrence."

Mara stopped speaking to take a breath. She looked intently at me.

"You know him, don't you?" she then asked.

"Yes, casually," I answered softly.

"Yes, well, he knows a great deal about you and your family; he has a lot to do with my being here today," she said most sincerely.

Mara looked at me again and this time she smiled broadly and I smiled back. I realized then that she knew my secret.

"I've had a great awakening, Rachel. God has…somehow… transformed me. And it wasn't easy because I was a terrible wretch; no, don't object, it's true and I know it.

"When Randall left me, my world fell apart. I didn't have a clue he was having an affair; I couldn't believe he was capable of embezzlement and I never imagined he would abandon me and our children, but he did.

"It was unbearable…I wanted to run away and hide but I had my children to think of. I was too humiliated to allow my friends to help and I turned inward. Eventually, my feelings went from despair to anger to hatred; I thought God had let me down so instead of trusting him to get me through my time of tribulation, I allowed the fire of affliction to consume me.

"Work was my salvation; I needed to prove something to myself and those around me. I needed to prove I wasn't a failure even though I felt like one inside." Tears slipped slowly down Mara's cheeks; my heart ached for her because I understood so intensely how she felt.

Mara took a tissue from her purse and wiped her eyes before continuing.

"I met a nice man at work; his name is Everett Lawrence and he's been with Cohen Brothers for many years. He's patient, kind and understanding. His wife died ten years ago in a car accident; they never had any children and he's been alone ever since.

"Everett was a tremendous help to me when I reentered the work force; he helped me establish a client list and introduced me to the best vendors. The founding partners of Cohen Brothers were very particular about whom they chose to do business with and that legacy has been handed down through the succeeding generations. It's a family-owned business, but you already know that, I'm sure."

I smiled but said nothing.

"Several weeks ago a new customer came into the store; she asked me to find a particular piece of furniture for her: a buffet she had seen at a friend's house. She said it was exquisite and she wanted to have one like it; you can imagine my surprise when she told me you were that friend.

"Well, after she described the piece to me, I went to Everett and asked him if he knew who the manufacturer might be or where I might obtain one like it. I was even more astounded by his answer.

"'If your friend saw an exquisite buffet at the home of Rachel Elliott,' he began, 'then it must be from *The King's House Collection*, which I know you're familiar with. What you probably haven't realized, however, is that the man who created that particular line, Theophilus Winthrope, was her grandfather; he was also the benefactor of our employer. Cohen Brothers exists today because of him.'"

"I couldn't believe it! We were friends for so many years and I didn't know!"

"Theophilus Winthrope, my grandfather, and the Cohens were very good friends," I began slowly. "They knew each other in Europe; my grandfather lived in France and the Cohens lived in a small town across the border in Germany.

"When my grandfather immigrated to America, he settled in Brooklyn, New York where he opened his first furniture store. I can't remember all the details but after he designed his own line of furniture, which he called *The King's House Collection*, he renamed his business and called it *The King's House Furnishings and Antiques*. The Cohen Brothers, while they remained in Germany, assisted him immensely in procuring many of the pieces he imported into America.

"When Hitler came to prominence, my grandfather advised the Cohens to leave Germany; they did with his assistance. He even gave them the financial backing they needed to open their own interior design business. They were lifelong friends and associates; I still communicate with their grandchildren who remain on the East Coast."

"Amazing!" Mara responded. "I've been dealing with The King's House for years and never realized you were connected to it. And then, when Everett told me Theophilus Winthrope was your grandfather and that he and the Cohens were good friends, everything became clear; my job didn't just fall into my lap like I thought, did it? You don't have to tell me, Rachel, I know that you opened the door for me.

"It's been difficult facing the truth about myself," she said relaxing a little. "Seeing you so happily married to Christopher made me insanely jealous, I'm not sure why, because you were always kind to me," she said contritely. "I don't deserve your friendship, but I'm here asking you to be my friend regardless. I can only hope that you'll give me another chance to prove myself more faithful in the future."

I reached over and clasped her hand warmly; nothing more was needed.

"I feel so blessed," she said wiping the tears from her eyes. "Everett's a great guy and my kids respect him; he's decided to adopt them. We're all going to have new names; I've even begun using my middle name: it's Aimee. I don't want to be Bitter Mara anymore; God has put a new song in my heart and I want to sing it with great joy.

Chapter Thirteen

A Mystery in Denmark

*O*n my return trip to Charlotte's home I made several attempts to contact Chris by telephone but I was only able to reach his message service. We were almost back to my daughter's home when he finally returned my call. I loved hearing the sound of his deep, melodious voice.

"I miss you," I confessed softly.

"I miss you, too," he replied warmly.

"Have you been out looking at locations again?" I asked, knowing how particular he could be.

"Yes, but I didn't like what we saw," he confessed and then went on to say that things were not progressing well. Finding just the right location for his new movie, a suspense thriller, was becoming extremely complicated.

"We don't want this movie filmed on a set; we want this production to have a certain 'feel' to it," he explained. "The main character's hometown needs to be picturesque but intriguing and a little obscure since it sets the tone for the mystery that follows."

We shared ideas about other possibilities and then I told him of my incredible visit with Mara and the amazing conversation that ensued. We kept our discussion brief knowing we would be home together soon where we could talk at length while alone.

My last evening at Charlotte's was filled with the simple delights of taking care of a household filled with children. She prepared a delicious rack of lamb for dinner, complete with white baby potatoes, sauerkraut, carrots and peas. When we finished, her little family orchestra performed several musical selections as entertainment: they really were very good. E.J. and Eliza both played the violin accompanied by their mother on the piano and their father on the cello. The twins had begun their musical careers quite early since both their parents were teachers and musicians. Edgar started them on the violin at three and when they turned five Charlotte began teaching them the piano; eventually they would learn the cello and if their interest allowed they might study the bass or viola. Ethan told his Papa he wanted to play the drums, which made Charlotte wince and Edgar smile.

Ethan, who was still a bit young, sat on my lap clapping his hands frequently and cheering loudly for his family. The selections my young grandchildren performed were modified versions of more complex pieces scaled down for young artists. Nevertheless, they were wonderful.

When the recital was over Charlotte served warm pieces of razzleberry pie topped with French vanilla ice cream. It was a heartwarming end to a charming visit.

After a light breakfast the following morning, I said my goodbyes and headed for home. E.J. and Eliza waved at the door and Ethan cried for Grandma as his mother cuddled him in her arms.

Driving along the highway on my trip home, my eyes fell upon the beautiful flowers in bloom along the coast. Ice plants growing on sandy flats were in abundance; the Sea Fig, a particular favorite that bloomed between April and October, had large deep reddish-lavender flowers that only opened in the full sun.

When I finally stepped from the car onto the driveway at the front of the estate, I breathed in the lovely fragrance of freshly cut grass spiked with the aroma of roses. The flowers and fruit trees in abundance on the estate were all in bloom. The hummingbirds, the tiniest of all birds, were profuse today. Mesmerized by their beauty

I watched while their strong wings kept them suspended in the air so their long beaks could reach down into the flowers to feed on the sweet nectar. I smiled and listened to the sweet song of the sparrows as they chanted from the trees above as if welcoming me back home.

Christopher opened the front door moments after I arrived; he was carrying Baby in his arms and both greeted me affectionately with warm, moist kisses. I hugged him, gently petted her fur and then laced my arm through his as we headed indoors toward the kitchen so I could greet Martha and Patricia.

"How 'bout a nice cold glass of freshly squeezed lemonade?" Martha said when we entered her domain.

"Sounds great!" we replied in unison. I walked to the pantry and got Baby a treat, which she gobbled down quickly and then scurried off down the hall to get a toy to play with.

"Lunch will be ready shortly, Mum," Martha said knowing I was always famished after a long drive. "Would you like it out on the terrace today?" I answered in the affirmative.

Chris and I went out the French doors that led to the patio and sat down at a table to sip our glasses of lemonade; it was a bit tart, just the way I liked it.

"Rachel, something interesting has happened since we spoke yesterday," my husband began slowly. His eyes were twinkling so I knew something was up.

"Really!" I said, afraid to ask what it might be.

"I got a call from Gabe Shomer this morning; he's in London at the moment but heading for Denmark shortly; he asked me to join him and Ralph there when I can.

"In Denmark? What's in Denmark, Chris?" I said, raising my eyebrows in wonder; knowing that if it involved the Shomer twins I might not like the answer.

Gabe and Ralph Shomer were handsome twin brothers; they worked for Interpol and I sarcastically referred to them as the European associates of my husband's movie alter ego, Secret Agent Ian Bruce. They were tall men standing over six feet four inches, with beautiful blue eyes and wavy dark blond hair. Their fair skin was dotted with freckles and their thick, square-set jaws gave them a rather intimidating look. Personally speaking, they exuded a tender boyish charm, which made them *almost* irresistible.

"What's in Denmark?" I said again, looking steadily into my husband's steel-gray eyes.

"A mystery it seems," he replied casually. "Actually, I spoke to James after hearing from Gabe and told him that I was planning on making the trip a fact-finding mission; it may be a perfect location for the new movie," he said with a wink and a smile.

"What about Spain?" I said with a grin.

"Spain is still a possibility," he replied. "We'll see."

I remained silent knowing that even though I had numerous questions running through my mind, he probably couldn't answer them.

Gabe and Ralph Shomer had come to our assistance when we needed help tracking down the individual who had been secretly stalking me. It wasn't until then that I found out about some of the clandestine activities my actor-husband was employed in.

"My *work* with the British Government," he began that night some months ago, "consists of little more than entertaining, on occasion, important foreign dignitaries. My celebrity status avails me opportunities others lack; I have access to individuals that might feel compromised meeting with or speaking to government officials. They are not, however opposed to sharing some rather intimate thoughts with an insignificant emissary such as myself. I'm not a *secret agent* by any stretch of the imagination; just an envoy of sorts conveying messages of benevolence between two parties." It was a little frightening knowing he was involved in international politics, regardless of how innocent a part he played.

"When will you be leaving?" I asked, not wanting to see him go so soon after my return.

"I'll wait until after the Fourth of July party and parade," he responded. "I couldn't possibly miss being with my family for those festivities…not even for the Queen!"

Martha brought our lunch outside; she had made chicken salad sandwiches, her specialty. The salad included chunks of chicken breast with sliced roasted almonds, dried cranberries and fresh rosemary in a creamy mayonnaise dressing deliciously served on sourdough bread. Slices of raw carrots, celery sticks and olives and a light green salad rounded out the afternoon meal; lemon cookies were a sweet dessert.

We talked through lunch; Chris told me all he had been busy doing while I was away and then I shared more about my week visiting with the family and friends. We separated after lunch so I could take care of my correspondence, which was piled high on my desk, and he could make some business calls.

I worked alone at my desk in the study; Chris worked upstairs in the office that Wesley normally inhabited on the third floor in the south wing. He told me he planned to meet Wesley in London so they could travel together to Denmark and then come home. Vianca would be pleased.

Wesley had been gone for some time and his new fiancé missed him terribly. We still hadn't decided what we would do when Wesley and Vianca married; he and his bride could continue to live with us at the estate but then Vianca would have to give up her job in the city. Or they could move back to Santa Monica and Wesley could work with her in the city and we could hire a new assistant to work at the estate with us; it was still yet to be decided. We were completely surprised by the pairing of the two: one an introvert and the other an extrovert, but they seemed incredibly happy and that was all that mattered.

My personal correspondence took a few hours to finish and when it was completed I used my computer to survey world news; after reading through a few interesting articles I decided to run an Internet search of foreign newspapers carrying recent articles on Denmark. There were several written about Tom Kristensen, a Dane who made history at Le Mans when he won his record seventh win, a fact I already knew. And there were a few regarding the crown prince and princess, who were expecting a baby, but I knew that as well.

Queen Margrethe II, a very progressive monarch, was hosting an art show; Chris, who had attended others in the past, told me she was quite an accomplished artist. Nothing else was new or exciting; certainly nothing appeared mysterious.

I turned off my computer and sat back in my chair trying to relax, but my mind constantly wandered back to Chris's words, "A mystery it seems." Was it a riddle?

Wait! I jumped up from my chair so suddenly I scared Baby who was silently sleeping at my feet.

"Sorry!" I said petting her head and then I turned and quickly walked into the hallway and up the staircase to my bedroom; Grandfather's desk was there. I opened the tiny cabinet door located on the top right side and removed his old black leather Bible, which was faded and frayed in places.

Carefully, I opened the book and found the passage I was looking for with Papa's notes written in the margin. His writing was faint but still legible; Papa wrote, "Hitler was not the one!" The text was from 2 Thessalonians; I read silently Paul's words, written to this young first-century church; they had been outlined in red ink by my grandfather:

> *For the mystery of iniquity doth already work: only he who now letteth will let, until he be taken out of the way. And then shall that Wicked be revealed, whom the Lord shall consume with the spirit of his mouth, and shall destroy with the brightness of his coming: Even him, whose coming is after the working of Satan with all power and signs and lying wonders, and with all deceivableness of unrighteousness in them that perish; because they received not the love of the truth, that they might be saved. And for this cause God shall send them strong delusion, that they should believe a lie: That they all might be damned who believed not the truth, but had pleasure in unrighteousness.*[1]

The mystery of iniquity Paul referred to was a person; that knowledge gave me pause. Could the mystery in Denmark be a person as well?

---

[1] 2 Thessalonians 2: 7-12 KJV

∽ *Chapter Fourteen* ∽

Family Fun

Christopher appeared pensive during the days immediately preceding the Fourth of July weekend. We didn't speak of Denmark or his mission and I chose not to mention the text concerning the mystery of iniquity, more commonly known to our generation as the Antichrist. Papa's sober comments scribbled around the text weren't new, just forgotten over time, buried in my subconscious.

"We thought Hitler was the Antichrist," Papa would say when he spoke about the war. "He was evil, yes," he sighed sadly, "but one more evil than he is yet to come, Rachel, so be on your guard for he will deceive many."

His admonition had frightened me at the time, but as I matured I began to understand that I had nothing to fear as the warning was for those who chose to reject the truth.

Martha and Patricia were busy making preparations to be delightfully inundated by the family; they looked forward to the children's visits as much as Chris and I. The laughter of sprightly children made the house feel full and alive.

I hadn't seen Victoria and Allen in awhile and I couldn't wait to see how much their boys had grown and matured. Michael, my oldest and most sober grandchild, was now eight years old. His younger sibling, Riley Conan MacDonald, named after my only brother who had died as a child, would be six in September. Riley loved his big brother and tried to do everything Michael did regardless of how difficult. Their personalities were uniquely different but they had an extremely close bond: Riley was drawn to artistic pursuits much like his mother while Michael favored scientific and philosophical endeavors like Allen.

It took two whole days for the house to fill with our adult children and grandchildren who arrived at different intervals, and as usual the noise level increased significantly with each new addition.

"Riley, you've grown an inch or two, haven't you?" I asked, giving my grandson a kiss on the cheek. Victoria's family was the last one to arrive home.

"I'm almost as tall as you are, Grandma," he squealed with delight.

"Almost, but not quite!" his mother said while giving me a hug. "Hi, Mom," she sighed, "it's good to be home for awhile."

Victoria walked slowly upstairs toward the rooms she inhabited with her family when they were here; she looked tired and a bit depressed.

The estate my grandfather had built so many years before was exceptionally large; it had three levels and a basement. Christopher and I lived on the second floor in the north wing in my grandparent's old rooms, which faced the ocean. Most of the guest rooms we used were on this level but when the house was full we used some of those located on the third floor as well.

Charlotte, who was coming downstairs while Victoria was going up, stopped to greet her sister on the stairway. They spoke softly for a few moments and then parted and Charlotte continued her trek down the long winding staircase in my direction.

"What's wrong with Victoria?" she asked when she reached me in the foyer.

"I haven't a clue?" I replied. "But if she wants to talk, she will. Let's see if Martha needs any help in the kitchen."

"Okay," she said with a smile as we walked away together.

The kitchen was jam-packed full of people when we entered;

men and boys surrounded the big oak dining table normally used by the staff. It was covered with sugar cookies elaborately decorated with colorful designs; Martha had baked the large round confections during the week and then she and Patricia spent an evening together frosting them.

"Hey," Charlotte said brusquely, "how come we weren't told cookies were being served?" she asked with a sarcastic smile.

"Sorry, Mama," Ethan said with a big grin. His mouth and tongue were covered with bright red frosting and he gently chose a pretty pink cookie with large white dots and handed it to his mother with a smile.

"Thank you, darlin'," she said giving him a kiss on the head and then a hug. He giggled and said, "You're welcome!"

Chris, Edgar and Scott were drinking coffee, munching on cookies and talking sports. Devon was sitting at the table with Dari and Eliza discussing their colorful confections while Chloe and Caitlin listened to E.J. as he shared which *colors* of frosting he thought *tasted* the best.

"Who wants to go to the beach for a swim?" Charlotte asked when the room became quiet. Several "I do's" resounded loudly around the room. While the adults were making plans for their excursion to the seashore, Victoria, Allen and the boys entered the kitchen.

"Cookies, Riley!" Michael said to his brother, "Come on." The two boys found a seat at the table next to their cousins and after asking permission, helped themselves to a cookie. Martha poured two more glasses of milk and asked Victoria and Allen if they wanted coffee or something cold.

"Nothing for me, thanks, Martha," Victoria said softly while Allen got a mug for coffee.

"I love your cookies, Martha," Allen said, "but I really need to watch my waistline; I'm getting a little portly."

"*Portly?*" Charlotte laughed, "Now there's an ancient word." Everyone laughed out loud and Allen pointed his finger at Charlotte in mock warning. Never one to back down, Charlotte continued to stir the pot and said, "Just do what Mom does, and walk *thirty* or *forty* miles a week." Allen rolled his eyes at his sassy sister-in-law and with hands placed on his hips he responded with, "Thanks, Charlotte, I'll be sure to do that."

"It's true," I said casually, "walking does keep your bones healthy and your heart strong. I walk about five or six miles a day except when I'm out of town."

The children ran upstairs to put their bathing suits on while their parents gathered up some drinks and snacks for their trip to the beach. Chris asked Patrick to pack up the beach umbrellas and chairs while I spoke to Martha about dinner.

"Rachel," Chris said as he headed out the door, "how soon will you be ready to leave?" he asked with a grin meant to help push me out the door. And I wondered who the real kids were in the group: the children or the men.

It was a perfect day for the beach—bright and sunny but not too hot. I sat on the warm sand under a large colorful umbrella watching my grandchildren swimming in the surf. Chris and Edgar were with the older children while Chloe and Charlotte remained close to the shore with the smaller ones. Devon and Scott and Allen were busy building sand castles and Victoria was reading a novel; it was perfect.

I lay back and closed my eyes to listen to the waves beating upon the shore and the laughter of my family playing in the surf. I loved the feel of the warm brown sand; the gulls flying overhead squawking at one another reminded me of other summer days spent here—some happy, some sad. When the sunlight began to fade, the air grew brisk and windy and the surf began to churn more voraciously; it was time to go home.

Martha had planned a dinner that she hoped would please the children she loved so much: hamburgers, hot dogs, skillet-fried potatoes and baked beans and ice cream topped with sliced bananas and strawberries and then covered with chocolate syrup for dessert. "One day without vegetables won't hurt them," she said when telling me the dinner menu. I had to agree. Our afternoon activities had certainly made everyone hungry and parents along with their children quickly cleaned up their plates.

We played a game of charades on the patio and then sang a few songs accompanied by Edgar who played the guitar. Dari, who had a lovely voice, even sang a Hebrew song she had learned in school. It was a perfect ending to a pleasantly delightful day.

The house was finally peaceful and quiet once everyone

retired; Chris and I were the last to go upstairs. We had just fallen asleep or so it seemed when the telephone rang; I looked at the clock beside my bed and saw that it was two A.M.

"Who was it?" I asked after Chris hung up the telephone.

"It was Pastor Edwards," he said climbing out of bed in a hurry. "The church is on fire."

Chapter Fifteen

The Fires of Sorrow

Chris dressed quickly and then awoke Scott and Patrick; as soon as the others were ready they drove to the church parsonage to meet John Edwards. Chris told me before he left that Sarah Edwards and her two sons, J.J. and Jude, were on their way to our home where they would stay the night.

Patricia got up with Patrick and immediately went to prepare rooms for the Edwards family while I awoke Martha; together we made coffee and sandwiches for those who would be returning to the estate as it was bound to be a long evening.

When Sarah arrived at our door she was visibly shaken; the boys, terrified, clung tightly to their petite mother. I ushered them into the parlor where they quietly huddled together on one of the large overstuffed sofas. Still dressed in their bedclothes, I had Patricia bring in a few blankets and pillows for the boys. Perhaps, when they felt secure, they would be able to fall asleep.

Martha brought large cups of hot honey milk for the boys and tea for Sarah and me. We didn't talk about the fire or its cause in front of her sons; that discussion would take place later and in private. We simply catered to their physical needs, giving each person whatever was necessary to help them decompress from the traumatic events of the evening.

Sarah Edwards had been a close personal friend for many years; she was one of those genuinely kindhearted people everyone loved. A violin in the orchestra of life she played the sweetest music. Sarah was a petite woman, thin and sprite; she had an elfish quality about her perhaps due to her short curly hair and small pointed chin; or maybe it was simply her magical smile that somehow inspired others to service and selflessness.

The Church of the Open Door, which Sarah and John Edwards had pastored for several years, was empty and closed when I returned home to live at my ancestral estate. John, who was then working as a pastoral counselor in a nearby community, had seen the vacant church and felt a burden to reopen it. He committed himself to prayer for God's guidance and eventually decided he would open the church if Sarah was agreeable. When she gave her consent they went to their denomination for approval and support, which they received; the church had been a thriving asset to the community ever since.

The parsonage was old and small when the Edwards moved into the tiny but comfortable two-bedroom residence, situated at the rear of the church property; eventually, both buildings had been refurbished and enlarged to care for the needs of their small family and our growing community.

We rested in the parlor for some time drinking our tea without speaking. Jude took only a few sips of his milk and weary of all the turmoil, eventually fell asleep; John Junior, the eldest of the two, was too anxious to sleep and remained alert huddling close to his mother until his father arrived with Christopher and Patrick.

"Luther Calvin and Julio Espinoza will be joining us shortly," Chris said giving me a quick kiss as he entered the room. His clothes smelled strongly of smoke and he was covered with soot. "Scott is still at the church; he called in the story to his editor and decided to stay a while longer to conduct interviews.

"How will he get home?" I asked calmly.

"I told him to call me and I'd send Patrick back but he declined; he said he'll catch a ride with someone or take a taxi," Chris softly responded.

"Do you want to meet in the small dining room?" I asked my husband once we had a moment alone. "Martha and I made coffee and sandwiches."

"That would perfect, Rachel" he said thankfully. Moments later Luther and Julio, who served as church elders along with Chris, arrived. Chris escorted the gentlemen into the dining room for refreshments while John accompanied his family upstairs to their rooms. He carried Jude in his arms while J.J. clung tightly to his mother's hand; once the boys were in bed John returned leaving Sarah, who was physically and mentally fatigued, upstairs with her boys.

I remained in the parlor while the men conversed in the dining room and eventually fell asleep in my chair; when I heard the front door open I awoke with a start to see Chris and John saying good-bye to Luther and Julio; it was sometime after sunrise.

"Don't worry, John," Luther said before closing the door, "everything will be ready for church services tomorrow morning; you can count on us." The men shook hands and departed; and John went upstairs for a shower and a little rest.

Luther Calvin, an African-American man, owned his own landscaping business and had lived and worked in the community for many years. Julio Espinoza was an emigrant from Guatemala; he had lived in California for the past ten years, five of which he and his family had spent as members of our church. They were both honest and reliable individuals and good friends to us and the Edwards.

"How bad is it?" I asked Christopher when we were finally alone. He and I climbed the stairs to our bedroom arm in arm.

"It's not a total disaster," he began, "but there's a fair amount of damage. John told me when he called that it was arson; what he didn't say until we arrived was that it was caused by a torch made in the shape of a cross. There were swastikas painted on the garage door and parsonage, and the number 666 was spray painted on the asphalt in the parking lot."

"Oh, no, Chris; you mean that it's a hate crime?"

"Perhaps…or it may be something worse!"

"What could be worse?" I asked without thinking.

"The Jewish Synagogue was burned down too, Rachel," he said

with a tired voice, "and pentagrams were spray painted on the cars in their parking lot."

"The occult?" I asked rather shocked.

"Perhaps!" he replied.

Later that afternoon, law enforcement investigators came to the estate to speak to Pastor Edwards. They laid out their assessment of the situation and told us that both fires were being categorized as hate crimes, something virtually unheard of in our area.

After dinner, Chris had an informal family meeting to brief the children about all that had transpired the evening before; he wanted them to prepare their children for what they would see the following day when we attended church. We were adamant that life continue as normal; we weren't about to give into terror.

We arrived for services earlier than usual on Sunday; it was a beautiful summer morning, with perfect summer weather. The long, white panels of linen fabric that made up the tent that formed our temporary church swayed gently in the cool, crisp breeze as we drove into the parking lot; Luther and Julio had managed to get it set up as promised. White folding chairs sat neatly underneath the linen, which provided us with shelter from the vibrant rays of the sun. Gay sprigs of summer flowers graced the table now serving as our altar in this temporary sanctuary; the tall white podium was decorated as well.

I pushed back tears when I looked at the remains of our scorched church; fortunately, only the front of the parsonage was damaged. Time and money would replace those things lost in the fire but the emotional wounds inflicted upon the minds of the inhabitants would linger indefinitely.

Pastor Edwards and Sarah stood, as usual, at the entrance to our provisional structure, smiling and greeting congregants as they arrived. The Sunday school teachers were busy setting up the children's tent and I was pleased to see J.J. and Jude happily acting as their helpers.

The early morning service was filled and even overflowing; not only were our regular congregants in attendance, but a healthy amount of curiosity seekers were here along with members of the press.

The first praise chorus sung that morning was one of thanksgiving; the inspirational music echoed sweetly in the open air.

Singing songs of gladness eased the heart and enabled the mind to soar high above the here and now helping us to set aside the pain of our current sadness and focus our attention on the Almighty. When John finally walked to the podium to greet the membership, a feeling of great anticipation seemed to permeate those who were in attendance that morning.

"Ladies and gentlemen," he began slowly, "today is a beautiful day. God is great and greatly to be praised." The congregation agreed with him and hearty "Amens!" echoed all around us.

"When I look into your faces I see the warmth of your love; in the past few days many of you have given selflessly of your time to assist me and my family and this church; we owe you a debt of gratitude and we offer you our sincere thanks." John quietly wiped the corners of his eyes before continuing. "God is good, my friends," he said and the congregation replied with, "All the time."

"When you look at the remains of our old church building you might be tempted to feel anger or despair, but I pray that you will join me in seeing the challenge that has been set before us; it is, I believe, an opportunity for spiritual growth and refinement. God allows us to go through the fires of life, my friends, because it is in the furnace of affliction that he removes that which offends and transmutes the remainder into something infinitely higher. We must step wisely and choose the course of action that will lead to our purification; otherwise, I fear we will be consumed.

"Where do we begin? is the first question we must ask ourselves. And the answer is: we must begin with forgiveness. It must be extended to those hopeless individuals, whoever they may be, that have caused our agony and pain and left us feeling vulnerable. And in spite of the vulnerability we face in this life, we who know Christ are secure in his love and never without hope for our lives are hidden in his.

"Beloved, we must join with the Apostle Paul and not be overcome by evil; but we must work to overcome evil with good. And we must follow the admonition of the Apostle John and walk in the light of the revelation that we have received.

"In preparing for this message today I asked the Lord to help me understand why anyone would want to destroy our church; I asked him as well the purpose of our suffering. Perhaps, some of you have been tempted to ask him the same questions.

"His answer surprised me: it was rather simplistic. I believe he said that we have all, at least to some extent, failed to fulfill our commission. We who walk in the light are called to share the love of God with those who live in darkness; and yet all too often we fail to even attempt to interact with those outside our system of beliefs. We have grown indifferent to the condition of humanity, and the reason is that we are more concerned with our own personal comfort than we are with the care of lost souls." Pastor Edwards stopped speaking to allow his words to penetrate the minds and hearts of the congregation; everyone was painfully silent.

"Please don't be angry with me," he implored. "I include myself when I say that the church has become overly complacent. Thousands of souls are swept into eternity every minute of every day and we act as though it doesn't matter; and perhaps to some of us, it doesn't!

"Well, friends, it needs to matter from now on! We are living in perilous times and we cannot afford to be self-satisfied any longer. We need to look within to see if we are really as rich and well off as we believe; and I think if we apply the salve of Holy Scripture to our eyes and look at ourselves honestly, we will see that we have been wretched and poor, naked and blind to our true spiritual condition.

"The Church of the Open Door exists for a reason; we are here to be a beacon of light shining in men's darkness; we are here to bring the truth of God's love to those who have never known it. And what the devil desires to use for evil, God can use for good if we let him. So, let us arise my friends from the ashes of our spiritual slumber and open our ears that we might hear what the Spirit is saying to the church: I think he is saying, 'Be zealous and repent.'"

It was a sobering message, one that touched us deeply. And when John ended the service with a call for revival people streamed forward for prayer.

"Before we leave this morning's service," John said in conclusion, "we need to consider our Jewish neighbors who also lost their place of worship. I spoke with Rabbi Abrams to offer our condolences and prayers; he said their small community will find rebuilding very difficult. Therefore, I'm going to ask our ushers to come forward so we might take a special offering to help them in their time of need."

At all three services that morning, John preached the same sermon and received the same general outcome. There were a few who were angered by his comments; some would not return. It was obvious, however, that the vast majority accepted his assessment because at dinner that evening he told us the collection taken for our Jewish neighbors was one of the largest ever received.

Chapter Sixteen

The Parade

Our first Fourth of July Parade was a big event for our small community; we, in particular, were anxious to attend as an equestrian unit from Noah's Ark had been entered. Christopher, who was the Grand Marshall, would be riding his new mount, Charlemagne, a stellar Thoroughbred from Kentucky.

Milky Way, Christopher's prize stallion, had passed away; the hand carved wooden statue of his image remained in our study, near a picture of grandfather's Ebony Bright, a black American saddle horse he had owned almost half a century before. The two men were amazingly alike in so many ways and shared many similar interests; no wonder I loved them both so well.

John and Sarah and the boys remained with us at the estate while looking for temporary housing; it was difficult being away from their home and congregation but we worked together to make their stay as enjoyable as possible. Julio had agreed to search for a temporary church facility with available office space until our facilities were repaired; as lovely as it was holding services outdoors we couldn't remain under the tent forever.

John, a truly holy man, was a different person after the fire; and his rather "seat scorching" sermon had rallied many members of the congregation to pull together and shift the focus of their energies and resources in a new area: reaching the lost. I began to wonder if the fire hadn't been a blessing in disguise. People seemed more joyful and productive in spite of the fact that the church had almost been destroyed, the parsonage was damaged, and our newly purchased school building was under repair due to the earthquake. God is Amazing!

The children sang joyfully as we drove along the highway headed into town; we left the estate early and traveled in a caravan of cars to the parking lot reserved for participants and guests. Security precautions necessitated our being in reserved seats slightly isolated from the general public and the section we were assigned to had a wonderful view of the parade route.

I watched from the sidelines high above the roadway as members of the community made their way along the parade route eagerly seeking out the perfect spot with the best vantage point possible to view the event. The crowd was quite large and people of varying shapes and sizes streamed by us; they were beaming with delight, eager to celebrate the Fourth of July festivities. Vendors milled about selling popcorn, peanuts and cotton candy and Coke.

"Who wants cotton candy?" I yelled out to those seated around me and a chorus of "I do's" quickly rang out; Allen graciously walked over to the vendor to make our purchases.

Minutes passed, the noisy crowd grew restless until the first faint sounds of music filled the air; louder and louder it became until our eyes finally rested on the members of our local high school band as they approached from a distance. The earth began to vibrate with the thunder of the drums as young men and women, gaily clad in colorful uniforms, marched by; skillfully they played their instruments producing patriotic tunes we could easily hum along to.

We smiled, laughed and cheered as the bandleader directed his troops; he was handsomely dressed in a bright white coat with big gold buttons. His tall white hat, sporting a fluffy white feather, glistened in the sun while his long golden baton kept beat for the marchers following behind. Row by row the musicians passed by and E.J., eager to share his knowledge, identified every instrument. There were trombones and saxophones, clarinets and oboes, piccolos and flutes, and sousaphones; the percussion instruments followed at the end.

Christopher appeared next riding on the back of Charlemagne; he looked splendid dressed in a pale blue cotton shirt and blue denim pants and jacket. The equestrian unit from Noah's Ark followed and had the distinctive honor of displaying our state and national flags. How proud I felt as I saw them ride by waving to all of us from their mounts.

Impatiently, the crowd turned back to see what would be next. This time we were entertained by a festive float decorated in red, white and blue. Lovely ladies and elegant gentlemen were fancily dressed in patriotic fashions; they smiled and waved as they passed by. We applauded loudly to display our pleasure and once again our eyes followed with joy as the float proceeded down the road out of sight; and so the parade continued.

The crowd was steeped in enthusiasm, greatly enjoying every aspect of the parade; it was a beautiful day to be outdoors enjoying the freedoms we so often took for granted. We cheered when the Salvation Army band passed by, knowing the good work they did in our community and the world at large. Another equestrian unit followed slowly behind them with men and women dressed in Spanish motif. Charlotte and I were extremely impressed by the beading on their costumes, not noticing until they passed that the parade had come to an end.

"Is that all?" Dari asked puzzled.

"I don't think so," I replied. "Something must have happened."

We sat in our seats patiently waiting for the next participant but no one came forward. Finally, an announcement was made over the loudspeaker asking us to be patient; a float had broken down.

Conversation broke out among the spectators who were eager to give their suggestions about what should happen to the broken down float. A few believed it should be towed so we could enjoy it but others suggested it be parked and left on the side of the road. Eventually, a decision was made, and the float was towed so the parade could continue. Those units ahead of the float, unaware of the delay, continued their journey without looking back; their goal was to reach the finish line and so they pressed on.

The casual spectator, I observed, was too overwhelmed and preoccupied by the excitement of the moment to detect a helicopter flying overhead. Distracted by the noise it generated, I watched as it observed us from above. "We called them 'whirlybirds' when I was young," I said pointing to the helicopter and speaking to Dari who was sitting next to me; she politely nodded.

"The pilot must be able to see all of us, and everything, just like God!" she replied and then turned to watch an assortment of clowns as they rode down the street on bicycles.

I stared at my granddaughter in awe; the pilot's view of the parade would have been vastly different from our own; his vantage point high above the crowd enabled him to see the event in its entirety; the beginning, the middle and the end, just as Dari had said.

He could see the spectators and participants at a glance; he knew where all the difficulties lay. When problems arose he wouldn't be caught off guard; and because of his position, he more than anyone else could offer the perfect solution for every situation.

My mind floated upward once again and as I eyed the helicopter, I smiled and then laughed within.

"What are you smiling at, Mom?" Charlotte, who was sitting on my other side, asked.

"Oh, nothing in particular," I replied. "I was just thinking how incredible God is; watching over us from up above."

"What made you think of that?" she asked, wrinkling her nose as she often did when confused.

"Oh, I don't know," I said with a smile. "Just a little birdie, I guess."

Chapter Seventeen

Pressing On

Sitting in the sun, watching from the sidelines, I began to consider Dari's comment. The whirlybird was still overhead and mentally placing myself in the pilot's seat I began to look at life from his perspective.

The multitudes of people on the ground below were divided into two categories: there were parade spectators and there were parade participants. The spectators were those sitting in the stands or standing on the sidelines: I chose to think of them as those who chose life apart from God. The participants, on the other hand, whether marching in the parade or working behind the scenes, I regarded as those who chose life united to God joined to one another with a common purpose: to use their gifts to serve him. Like the members of a band they had to work and play in harmony in order to make beautiful music.

Spectators and participants have a lot of things in common: they are ordinary people, regardless of gender, age, race or intelligence. They eat, drink, sleep, work and play. They experience joy, pain and heartbreak; they give and they take; they live and then they die. And they each become spectators or participants based on one common factor: one group accepts and the other group rejects God's offer of redemption.

Participants in the "Heavenly Kingdom Band" must put their faith in Jesus Christ as Savior and pledge their allegiance to him alone; in turn, they are given a clean new uniform, an instrument to play and a place in the ranks among their peers. And while each member marches together as part of a team, they still march as individuals, one by one, following the Bandleader who alone sets the pace as he directs the band.

My eyes traced the parade route remembering the band that had already passed, each member facing forward to finish the course.

And then my concentration broke as I recalled the float that had collapsed along the route; how similar to real life that incident was. Marriages fall apart just as mine had; children drift away, jobs are lost and friendships are destroyed; and sometimes we feel paralyzed by pain, or bogged down in grief, unable to move forward for awhile. And when we hear the suggestions of a thousand different voices, we need to be mindful to listen to only one: that which moves us closer to our goal.

The crowd applauded loudly as the last of the parade participants performed and moved on; spectators leaving the stands followed happily behind them on their way to their cars. We waited a while for the crowd to disperse and then gathered up our belongings, carefully shepherding the children toward the parking lot; once when I turned to look up I noticed the whirlybird still hovering overhead.

We didn't wait for Chris, who would be riding with the equestrian unit back to Noah's Ark where we would join them. We were all looking forward to an evening of fun and festivities at the ranch.

The members of Noah's Ark were housed at the ranch, under the watchful eyes of Eli and Susanna Samuels. Their forty years of work as licensed clinicians and their real life experiences had prepared them in a variety of ways to shepherd the young people now under their care. And since Noah's Ark was specifically created to redeem the lives of abused teens and neglected animals, we were overjoyed to see some of our residents riding in the parade as they were the first fruits of that endeavor.

A grand luncheon was served prior to the games and activities planned for our family, friends and employees. The grandchildren participated with gusto; Caitlin and Ethan, still a bit too young for some things, enjoyed an ice cream cone before going on a pony ride at the stable. The older children went with Christopher for a ride out on the open range; this was the highlight of their day and I was pleased to hear that their equestrian skills were progressing.

The teens that lived and worked on the ranch were referred to as team members because they were expected to act as a team, united to support one another in order to accomplish mutual goals. The ranch housed fourteen team members all under the age of nineteen. There were eight boys and six girls; all in varying stages of recovery. Genevieve, the youngest at thirteen, was a particular favorite. She had suffered terrible atrocities at the hands of her parents—such things that I shuddered to recall. Quiet and withdrawn when she arrived, she was beginning to blossom like a young rose springing up out of a patch of thorns.

A fireworks display brought the long day to an end; we were home within minutes, our tired children and their progeny eager for bed. Christopher and I, too excited to sleep, went into the kitchen for a cup of tea.

Martha, who had returned home earlier in the evening, was at her desk working on the menu for the week.

"Martha, my love," my husband said in his most endearing manner, "I'm pining for a cup of tea." Martha smiled at him and said, "And yer wouldn't mind a slice of my apple pie either, I expect!" She shook her head as she walked to the stove and turned on her whistling tea kettle. I grabbed some cups and a ceramic teapot from the cupboard and placed them on the table. Martha had already retrieved a fresh pie, forks and dishes and with obvious pleasure she began to cut us each a slice.

"This is delicious," Chris said taking a large mouthful. Martha only smiled; she was putty in his hands.

Moments later a few of the adults trickled into the kitchen until it was eventually filled.

"I thought you children were so tired you were going to bed!" I said grinning.

"Charlotte reminded us that Martha was going to bake pies today," Edgar said licking his lips.

"There's apple and peach," she sang out, quite elated that they approved. And in no time at all they were each munching on a piece of their favorite pastry. I looked around the room at my happy family; only Victoria was missing.

Allen was busy talking to Scott so I left the room in search of my missing child who I found sitting in the parlor alone.

"What's up?" I said taking a seat next to her on the couch.

"Nothing!" she replied feebly.

"Yes, something?" I said a little sternly. "Why don't you tell me what's troubling you?"

"It's nothing, really, Mom. You'll think I'm vain if I tell you. It's just…well…I hate to admit it but I think I'm feeling a bit *old*."

"Is that because your birthday's just around the corner?"

Victoria smiled, "Maybe, I don't really know for sure; that may be part of it. I just feel…well, when I get together with the family, I feel so useless in comparison to my sisters. Devon's a doctor, Charlotte's a teacher and I'm just a homemaker. I don't feel like I make a very valuable contribution to the world at large. Oh, I love being a wife and mother, and I love being a homemaker. There are times though, when…"

"When you're just a little bored! Right?"

Victoria heaved a sigh of relief, "Right, exactly. Oh, Mom, does that make me terrible?"

"Of course not!" I proclaimed vociferously. "Victoria, I stayed home with all you children; but I did have my fundraising and charity work as an emotional outlet. You have several of those; you work in your church and you have really great friends. Maybe, what you need right now, is something a little more stimulating," I suggested.

"Like what?" she asked plaintively.

"Oh, I don't know what in particular, just something to keep your mind active; something that will give you a sense of accomplishment. Have you thought of attending a lecture series, or joining a club?" Victoria looked disinterested. I remained silent for a few moments, thinking about the woman when she was a girl. What was it she liked to do then?

"Victoria, when you were in your teens, you began to paint a little. Do you remember? And you were good; you had definite talent but you had barely begun to develop that talent when you discovered *boys*." Victoria smiled and laughed.

"I did like to paint; it was fun," she agreed.

"Riley gets his artistic flavor from you; and you probably get it from Papa. You loved the art classes you took in college; you could take a few more. It may open a creative outlet for you; why don't you think about it?"

Victoria smiled and gave me a big hug; "Mom, you're the best!" she said with delight.

"Want a piece of pie now?" I teased and we walked back to the kitchen together.

Chapter Eighteen

Brood of Vipers

*T*he kitchen was still buzzing with people eating, drinking and talking when Martha turned on the small television set mounted on the wall so we could catch a few minutes of the evening news. The local station carried the highlights of the parade and after listening to the weather report, we switched over to a cable station to see what was going on in the world.

"And now for the latest juicy gossip straight from the horse's mouth," the reporter said with a malicious smile.

"Oh, let's turn on another station before she starts to whinny," Chloe said disgusted, "everything she reports is a distortion of the truth." Chris, who had the remote, was just about to switch stations when his picture appeared on the monitor.

"Here's the latest," the reporter began, "on the delectable Sir Christopher Elliott. These exclusive photos were taken today of him cavorting in the hills high above the Pacific Ocean with a beautiful playmate whose name is still a mystery. Is his marriage on the rocks? Let your eyes be the judge!"

Chris turned the television off; he was visibly angered.

"What a malicious fabrication!" he said, furious at the implications made.

"How did she get those pictures, Dad?" Chloe asked abruptly.

"Someone with a high powered photo lens could have easily taken them from the highway," Scott opined. "The photographer either waited until he had just Chris and this woman in the shot, or he took several pictures of the group out riding this afternoon and found one he could crop to get the desired result; it happens a lot, I'm sorry to say."

"It's reprehensible," I said looking toward my husband. "Maybe we should take legal action this time, Chris; it seems to be happening more and more frequently."

"As much as I detest these nasty reports, we need to act wisely and not in haste," he replied cautiously. "I wish I knew who was responsible because I don't believe it's this woman. What does she hope to gain by these attacks?"

"Do people need a reason to be cruel?" Scott asked. "Her pen name is Salacious Sally; and from what I've heard about her she can be pretty malicious," he interjected, "without a reason. One thing, she isn't is stupid; my understanding is she's been sued dozens of times and never lost a case; she may be unscrupulous but she's careful how she words things. You heard what she said: was there anything derogatory?"

"No, but it's the implication of her words that matters; in a way she's misrepresented the facts and in doing so she's damaged Chris's reputation. Isn't that what slander is?" I asked angrily.

"How has she misrepresented the facts? She displayed a picture of Chris and a woman riding in the hills; nothing wrong there. Then she states that the woman is a beautiful playmate but anyone you have fun with could be considered a playmate, so nothing wrong there either. She finishes by asking a question about his marriage. How can you accuse her of slander based on that?"

"But they weren't riding alone," Charlotte said, and added, "there were other people riding with them.

"That's true but she didn't say there weren't; and if someone sent her the pictures she might not even be aware of those facts," Scott quickly replied. "The truth is that Chris is a powerful man and all powerful men have enemies."

"Well, he's never been attacked like this before," I said, "so it's obvious that someone is out to either hurt him or discredit him and I'd like to know who and why."

"You both do so much good, I don't understand it," Victoria said sadly. "Why do people act like such snakes?"

"Serpents are cunning and malignant so you need to be prudent when you search for a single devil in a brood of vipers!" Allen said philosophically. He had been standing on the sidelines listening and interjected his thoughts for the first time.

"You have two choices in this situation: you either address it or you let it go. There will be ramifications either way, I'm afraid."

"Such as?" Victoria asked.

"If you address it, you draw more attention to it but you may stop some of the mudslinging," Allen began.

"Which is what we've been doing but the attacks have only increased over the past year!" I said solemnly.

"Well," Allen began again, "you could choose to ignore it, but it may only embolden the guilty and in the end invite more of the same."

"I'm not one to run away from a problem," Chris said wisely, "but I also don't need to defend myself. People have the freedom to think whatever they want to think about me; it's impossible to escape the censure of the world so I can't be overly sensitive to it. I must simply endeavor to do the right thing in any given situation; so let's leave it alone for now and pray before taking any course of action."

Those words brought the discussion to an end; Chris would go no further without devoting time to prayer first and I knew in the end his humble intercourse with God would help him ascertain the divine will, which he would obey without hesitation.

Chapter Nineteen

The Betrayer

*T*he answer to my righteous husband's fervent prayer came rather quickly through an unexpected but reliable source.

Vianca Bliss had worked for Christopher for some years in a multitude of positions; she was currently serving as his public relations assistant/director for his production company. A lovely lady in her mid thirties, Vianca was tall and thin with short brown hair; she was animated and energetic and her sparkling, sanguine personality enabled her to perform most of her duties with great satisfaction and joy.

She became acquainted with Wesley, Christopher's personal assistant, when their paths crossed recurrently in the line of work, and over a period time a strong friendship developed between them. It wasn't love at first sight for this particular pair; Wesley was too melancholy for anything that plebeian. Their love grew from mutual respect and admiration and while we were somewhat surprised when they announced their engagement we were also extremely delighted they had found one another.

Vianca was inundated with telephone calls from several friends

immediately following the evening news broadcast, which she
hadn't seen. She turned on the television and then watched a later
broadcast to catch the replay; due to the lateness of the hour she
waited until the following morning to call Chris.

His personal line rang shortly after eight; it was Vianca. We
were still in bed and while I only heard his half of the conversation
it was evident from the look on his face that he was exceedingly dis-
pleased. After saying thank you and good-bye, he related her side of
the conversation to me.

"Vianca saw the evening news telecast late last night," he began
slowly; "alerted to it by several friends. Since Wesley's out of town
she's been receiving all correspondence from the press and several
reporters have already called her asking for my comments. She of
course denied all of the allegations as usual but said that her real
cause of concern was over a different matter. Two weeks ago, while
having lunch in a restaurant in Westwood she said she saw this same
reporter having a conversation with…and mind you she isn't accus-
ing her of anything…but she was having a conversation with Jessica."

"Jessica?" I said stunned. "Jessica Todd?" I said a second time in
disbelief.

"Yes, Jessica Todd; she said she didn't think much of it at the
time because they were speaking to each other near the lavatory
facility and she thought they might have simply bumped into one
another. It may have been completely innocent, but she thought we
should know."

"But neither Jessica nor Paul were here yesterday," I explained.

"No, but they were invited. She and Paul are in Los Angeles and
they knew we were having a party."

"Still," I began defensively, "what would Jessica gain by stirring
up rumors about either of us?"

"Do you remember a few months ago there was gossip going
around about me and another woman at the studio? Before her it
was Violet Devries, and before that there was the innuendo that I
was a drunkard and then there was the gossip about you in that
magazine written about your health when you cut your hair. The
writer of that article specifically said all her information came from
a 'very reliable source.' Rachel, haven't we wondered about all these

things and more? Reporters and photographers have mysteriously appeared at several events no one knew we were attending—no one, except our family."

"But why would Jessica want to harm *us*? I've, we've, been extremely kind to her considering the circumstances."

"I don't have the answer to that question; I guess you'll have to ask her," Chris said frankly.

"You want me to call her?" I asked surprised. "How can I call her? What would I say? We have no evidence proving that she's done anything wrong."

"You need to call Paul," he said flatly, "and ask him."

Chris kissed me gently and excused himself; he dressed and left the room, having numerous business matters to attend to prior to departing for Denmark but I knew he also wanted to give me the space I needed to think and to pray.

I walked to the bedroom balcony, opened the doors and silently drifted outside. The ocean was peaceful and calm today, glistening like dark blue glass. I stood and watched it ebb and flow pondering the difficultly of my situation.

Jessica Kennedy-Brown, now Todd, had once been my rival. I remembered the first time we met; she was sitting in my kitchen, alone with Paul my first husband. Her presence made me shake inside as it confirmed my suspicions that something was seriously wrong between my husband and me.

She was a beautiful woman in her early thirties then—a widow with no children. Jessica was five feet ten inches tall, had beautiful iridescent blue eyes and natural blonde hair she still kept cut stylishly at the chin. She was intelligent and had a law degree; she was introduced to Paul by one of his subordinates who believed she would be a definite asset to their firm. She became much, much more and eventually Paul left me to marry her.

My life moved forward; Chris and I met and then married and we worked hard to maintain decent relations with Paul and Jessica, who became his wife. I had included her in many family activities for the sake of our children and grandchildren. Had that been a mistake? I didn't think so.

I left the balcony and walked back into my bedroom; sitting at Papa's desk I lifted the telephone receiver and dialed Paul's cell phone. He answered on the third ring; I hesitated and then quietly shared the events that had transpired the evening before. He had seen the telecast as well and expressed his regrets.

"Paul," I said slowly, "I have something else to add; something that's difficult for me to say, so please bear with me."

I went on to explain the events that transpired as related by Vianca; Paul seemed stunned.

"Rachel, I'm sure Jessica doesn't know this reporter. I find it difficult to believe that she would have anything to do with anything so grievous, but I promise I will ask her."

"I'm sorry, Paul. I hope this is a mistake of some sort; I hate having to ask you but I would appreciate it if you would call me back as soon as possible." Paul agreed and hung up the phone.

Chapter Twenty

Thought, Word, Deed

*T*wenty-four hours later Paul was standing at our front door; the guards in the security booth at the entrance to the mansion had announced his impromptu arrival, which gave me pause for concern. Christopher greeted him at the door and extended his hand in friendship; Paul grabbed it and hung on tightly. He was pale and trembling, sure signs things weren't good.

"How about a strong cup of coffee and something to eat," my gentle husband said quietly. Paul nodded his agreement without speaking and the three of us went into the small private dining room we used for intimate gatherings. I excused myself and went to the kitchen to speak with Martha and then returned to hear what Paul had driven so far to say; I was afraid of what it might be.

Martha entered the dining room a few moments later quietly pushing the tea cart laden with a pot of coffee and cups for the three of us, along with a platter of pastries and serving plates and utensils; she set the table without speaking and then quickly left the room.

Paul sat in silence but I could tell he was agitated; he was an unemotional man and took pride in the fact that he could remain uncommonly taciturn in the most difficult situations. This morning, however, his brow was covered by tiny beads of perspiration, his personal signature of stress that I had grown to recognize from our years together.

"I can't believe this has…has happened," he stammered eventually. "In a way, I feel responsible…not directly perhaps, but indirectly." He took a few sips of his coffee and settled himself a little before speaking again.

"I hate to have to confirm your suspicions about Jessica but they were correct. I sat down with her last night and questioned her about the photographs and articles written about you both over the past year or so. At first, she denied having any knowledge about the reports that have appeared in the press; and yet, strangely, I wasn't convinced. When I told her she had been seen speaking with the reporter in question, she became defensive and finally admitted that she knew her and for reasons she refused to reveal, she said she had agreed to provide her with some intimate details of your lives." Paul took a short break before speaking again to compose himself.

"I'm at a complete loss to explain her actions; it's possible they stem from jealousy or envy. I'm not sure it makes a difference why she did what she did; her behavior is indefensible but then who am I to judge." He closed his eyes momentarily closing out the world as he so often did when he had to face something extremely unpleasant.

Tears welled up in my eyes as he spoke and my heart ached. Jessica and I hadn't been close friends but she had been welcomed in our home and at our table, which made her duplicity that much more grievous. Our relations had been peaceful and friendly for many years and I wondered what had occurred to turn her against us.

"I have to admit," Paul began slowly, "that I always thought your grandfather was terribly old-fashioned," he said with a slim smile, "always sharing little snippets of his conventional beliefs. He warned me frequently to be mindful of my thoughts, words and deeds. I never really listened. You know what I'm talking about, don't you, Rachel?" he asked looking for a sign of recognition.

"Yes, I do," I replied as Chris looked my way and then waited for an explanation.

"Papa often said that all the Ten Commandments manifest themselves, to some degree, outwardly with the exception of the tenth, which deals with desire or coveting. He said that covetousness occurs in the mind and is the root of the other sins that manifest themselves in word or deed," I explained.

"I never appreciated his wisdom," Paul continued, "because it always seemed so archaic. And because I didn't listen to his sound advice we're all suffering!"

I sat in silence not knowing how to respond; Chris, sitting at the head of the table with Paul on his left reached over and placed his hand on his shoulder. He didn't say a word, just allowed the man time to deal with his emotions. When Paul finally regained his composure, he apologized.

"Life is very incongruous," he moaned meditatively.

"Sometimes," I solemnly replied.

"Well, if this scene isn't fantastic I don't know what is," he said tartly. "You and Chris consoling me, your former husband, over my wife's betrayal; the betrayer is, in the end, betrayed as well."

"What are you talking about?" I asked completely perplexed.

"I'm sorry, I'm being a little flippant I guess. I haven't told you everything: It seems Jessica is tired of being married to me; she said she's found someone younger to spend her time with and that she is filing for divorce."

"Oh, Paul, I'm so sorry!" I replied utterly surprised. "Perhaps, she'll change her mind."

"I doubt it; she seemed pretty determined," he said wearily. He had aged a great deal over the past several years and today he seemed terribly sad and alone.

There wasn't much more either of us could say but to express our sorrow. Paul sat quietly for a few moments more and then stood up to leave.

"I came here today to apologize in person for the grief we've both caused, and to let you know that I'll be taking steps to rectify the situation. You'll be seeing some sort of retraction in the press regarding all this nastiness; you have my word." He shook hands and turned to leave but then took a few steps back to say, "Please don't tell the children about Jessica; I'd like to do that myself." We nodded our agreement and he quietly departed.

Watching him leave was painful; I hurt for the man I once loved so dearly and in doing so I felt disloyal to Chris.

"It's okay," Chris said taking my hand in his and kissing it gently.

"What?" I responded.

"It's okay to feel sorry for him," he replied, "He was your husband for decades; you have a history together and a part of you still cares about his well-being."

"Were you just reading my mind?" I asked, surprised but relieved. When we left the dining room we were greeted by Charlotte, who had come downstairs for a cup of coffee.

"What's going on?" she asked with a worried look on her face. "I saw Dad leaving; is he okay?"

"Your dad is going through some difficulties at the moment, which he's asked us not to discuss. I'm sure he'll speak to you girls as soon as he's able." My words ended the discussion and Charlotte walked away carrying her cup carefully upstairs to check on her family. Christopher and I walked outside toward the chapel to pray.

Chapter Twenty-one

Earthen Vessels

The chapel was cool and dim when we entered; shadowy figures swayed back and forth on the walls provided by several tall trees swaying outdoors. The long willowy silhouettes, though silent, brought the noiseless room to life appearing as ethereal angels floating gently through the diffused light.

We made our way to the front pew where we normally sat when we came to pray, an almost daily occurrence. The chapel bells in the small tower above the structure tinkled lightly as the wind blew outside, and for reasons unknown I found its charming sound strangely comforting.

The octagonal building was tall; each of its eight walls stood ten feet high. Four of the walls were oak paneled. The other four held long panes of beveled glass in the shape of a hexagon. In the center of each hexagon was a beautifully decorated stained glass painting with an outside border painted in green to unify the design.

The floor was covered with exquisite white marble; eight pews, four on each side of the room with an aisle down the center, faced the altar. One octagonal aisle encircled the entire building.

The altar was situated directly opposite the two large oak doors through which we entered the room; it too was made of white marble and behind it was one of the oak-paneled walls. The stained glass window to the left of the altar was my favorite. An old wooden cross stood in a field of white lilies, a gentle lamb and majestic lion lying at its feet. A swath of deep purple linen hung over the limbs of the cross while rays of bright sunlight emanated from it onto the pale blue sky in the background.

The chapel had been completely renovated and was a lovely place to pray. The pews had been removed, sanded and varnished and then reupholstered in dark green velvet. Deep purple carpet runners decorated with a pattern of green ivy lined the aisle ways and one long strip of carpet ran behind the altar. Eight elegant crystal lamps hung from the ceiling above, one over each pew. A scarf of white satin edged in hand crocheted lace sat elegantly on the long altar adorned only with two silver candelabras.

I lit the candles as I always did when we entered to pray; we sat in silence for a time searching our hearts before entering into discourse with the Lord. Chris prayed first; his words were poignant, reflective and precise. His intuitive perceptions and his intrinsic awareness of man's nature enabled him to pray in a truly profound way.

Today, Chris acted as an intercessor for Paul and Jessica; he began by reminding the Father of man's fragility.

"Our earthen vessels are weak, Father, and therefore easily broken," he prayed with deep compassion. And he continued with a sincere petition that Paul would be strengthened in his hour of need.

"Why do you think Paul is so adamant in blaming himself for Jessica's behavior?" I asked him once we finished praying for the couple; we walked up the hill to spend some personal time together among the beauty of the fruitful orchard trees.

"Probably because inside he still feels guilty for committing adultery, and that may be part of the reason his current marriage is unraveling."

"They were both partners in the affair, Chris; don't you think she's just as responsible for her actions and choices as he is."

"Yes, Darling, I do," he replied softly, "but Jessica may not feel guilty about her actions or choices. Paul obviously does."

His comments were startling; I hadn't considered Jessica's feelings or lack of feelings of guilt about the affair. Paul had asked for forgiveness years earlier, which I had already granted to them both for my own peace of mind.

"Well, they're headed for rough waters," I said gazing across the landscape to take a peek at the deep blue ocean below; the waters were extremely choppy today and the air was fairly brisk.

"I agree and I'm sorry for them; they're both going to suffer."

Chris wrapped his arms around me and we stood together facing the seashore breathing in the fragrant air; it was filled with the light scent of citrus, and as always it was invigorating; being outside always made me thankful for the majesty of creation.

"You know, Chris, going through divorce is terribly painful," I said looking away, "but if Paul hadn't left me for Jessica, you and I wouldn't be together."

"Out of sorrow came something sweet," he said in his warm melodious voice. He snuggled his face into my neck tenderly and kissed me on the cheek and said, "You captivated my heart and with one look of your eyes I was smitten."

"You're a hopeless romantic, my love," I said with a smile.

"True, Darling, too true." We laughed and continued our lovely walk knowing it might be our last together for some time.

Chapter Twenty-two

Small Miracles

Christopher left for Denmark a few days later; his departure aroused a feeling of anxiety within me, perhaps because the purpose of his journey was unknown. I hated the mystery that surrounded the work he did for the British government but I knew he couldn't elucidate regardless of how much he wanted to; he was confined by his duty to his country and the personal ethics he maintained as a man of his word. Being in the dark, however, left me feeling weak and impotent; why, I wondered, did we think we could control what we understood?

Once again I found myself surfing the Internet looking for international news that might give me a clue about my husband's current mission. There were only two news events of any significant interest that involved Denmark. The first was of the President's interview on Danish television in which he discussed his refusal to sign the Kyoto treaty. And the second was a report that detailed his visit to the Scandinavian nation in which he thanked the Danes for their support of the war in Iraq and Afghanistan.

Christopher called when he landed at Heathrow Airport where

he was greeted by Wesley. The two were remaining in London for a few days and would then fly to Denmark and meet up with Ralph and Gabe Shomer. "Don't be surprised if all telephone correspondence ceases at that time," he said soberly and as a warning. "I'll contact you when I can but it may not be until we begin our journey back home." His words frightened me but I again remained silent.

Frustrated and bored, I sat alone at my desk in the study, going over some business matters. I read and reread the same sentence ten times from a letter a new vendor had written. It was just impossible to concentrate; my mind was too filled with other things. The ring of the telephone startled me but I welcomed the diversion.

"Hello," I said softly.

"Rachel, hi, this is Sophie." Her voice was filled with alarm and I quickly responded to it.

"What's wrong?" I had hardly spoken the question when her tearful response spilled out over the telephone line.

"My mother is seriously ill," she said now sobbing between words. "She just called to say she's been diagnosed with breast cancer."

"Oh, Sophie, I'm so sorry," I replied tenderly. "What can we do to help?"

"At the moment, nothing, thank you; but…I'm so sorry to have to do this but…"

"What is it, Sophie?" I asked, calmly trying to diminish her fears.

"Rachel, I'm afraid I'm going to have to leave; I don't want to resign, I love it here, but my mother needs me right now…" her words drifted off. Silence ensued.

"I'll be down in a few minutes," I said, "and we'll talk." I hung up the telephone, went into the kitchen to see Martha, called the chef at the inn and then headed down to Sophie's office.

When I arrived at the inn, a pot of tea and two mugs were waiting on a tray for me just inside the kitchen door. I placed the plate of cookies I had brought with me from Martha on the tray and then carried it up the stairs to the third floor where Sophie was waiting in the small office that was part of her quarters. Setting the tray down on a table, I gave Sophie a hug and allowed her to cry.

When her sobbing subsided, she sat down on her small sofa and I poured her a cup of hot tea; we both remained silent as we sipped the hot liquid that so often helped the body and mind assimilate life's woes.

Sophie had matured in her tenure at the inn, and while she was still something of an industrious perfectionist, the anger that once drove her to perform had been released; a more tranquil spirit now reigned within.

"It's amazing," she began when she was ready to speak, "that my mother needs me and wants me near, considering all the years we battled with one another, isn't it?"

"Amazing and wonderful at the same time," I replied. "You've both worked hard at overcoming your differences and together you've built a fairly good relationship."

"It's hard to believe there was a time when I thought my mother didn't love or approve of me.

"Oh, Rachel, I love my mother so much," she cried. "We had so many difficult years, and now that we're getting along so well, this happens."

"I know, Sophie, but isn't it wonderful that you'll be able to face this problem together? Do you remember the days when you thought you'd never measure up to your mother's expectations; and now you're practically her best friend!"

Sophie smiled and then laughed a little, "I tried so hard to be perfect because I wanted to please her; I think I was trying to win her love. And then whenever I failed to meet her expectations, I felt worthless and embittered. You helped me see that I needed to learn to be myself and give my mother the same freedom. It was very liberating for both of us; our relationship has grown because of it and that's a miracle."

"A lot of grace and a little space helps produce healthy relationships," I answered. "And realizing we can't control or change anyone but ourselves."

"I hate leaving here," Sophie said after we talked for a while. "I hate leaving you and my friends but I really don't have a choice. I need to help my mother."

"You can always come back if you want to," I replied. "And rest assured that Chris and I will help you in any way we can."

"I don't have to leave immediately," she finally concluded, not wanting to face the inevitable, "but I'll need to shorten my work week until a replacement can be found, if that's all right."

I hugged her good-bye after telling her not to worry and walked next door to the Tea Cottage to speak to Noah.

Sophie was too conscientious to leave us shorthanded but she needed to be free to care for her mother as quickly as possible; therefore, I asked Noah to begin training Sadie, our weekend innkeeper to become a provisional manager until we could find a permanent replacement.

The grandchildren were outside playing in the play yard when I returned home, and I joined my daughters on the patio for a refreshing glass of lemonade while we watched them play. Dari, Eliza and Caitlin were playing nicely in the girl's tree house while the boys played on the jungle gym.

The play yard area had been developed by Luther Calvin, our groundskeeper, as a safe place for our grandchildren to play when visiting us at the estate. A five-foot concrete border encircled an enormous sandbox built on a leveled area of terrain behind the estate, which was also utilized for bike riding.

A cedar play set was erected inside the sand box. There was a high gazebo in the center of the play set, which stood about five feet off the ground. The children loved to meet here; underneath the gazebo stood a small picnic table where they could eat their lunch. To reach the gazebo the children had to climb up a doublewide ladder on one side of the yard to a crow's nest and then cross over a small bridge. Leaving the gazebo from the opposite side the children would crawl through a large funnel to a second doublewide ladder. Underneath the bridge were swings and climbing ropes. There was a separate smaller activity center designed for toddlers with swings and a ladder just their size.

The girls and boys also had separate tree houses in a grassy area apart from but near the sandbox; we often roasted hot dogs and made s'mores over a small wood pit barbecue built in a safe area away from the trees.

"Where are the men today?" I asked the girls.

"They wanted to go riding," Victoria said quickly. "Chris has been trying to turn them into equestrians," she added with a snicker, "but not having much luck."

"Why do you say that?" Charlotte asked her older sister.

"Why, Char? Just watch Allen when he walks in later. He's fallen off his horse at least three times, and have you seen him in his cowboy hat and boots? Oh, my!" We all burst out in laughter.

Chapter Twenty-three

The Night Sky

*W*hen Allen, Edgar and Scott arrived home for dinner our attention was duly focused on all three. It was evident Allen was in pain and struggling to walk; it wasn't easy to keep from laughing when Edgar described his brother-in-law's most recent escapade with a horse. Allen laughed out loud when he boldly confessed, "Pastor Samuels told me he prays without ceasing the moment I enter the stable!" Poor Allen!

The hot day began to cool down when the sun slipped away and evening unfolded. Edgar, our chef, barbecued chicken on the large patio grill along with baked potatoes, corn on the cob, sweet peppers, squash, zucchini, and onions. Martha prepared several cold side dishes; her Greek pasta salad was delicious and besides a delectable green salad she prepared a fresh fruit salad combining melon, bananas, strawberries, raspberries and blueberries. Corn muffins and honey butter filled out our delicious summer backyard barbecue menu.

Michael, who had received an expensive new telescope for his birthday, set it up near the play yard in a small clearing where access to the night sky was best. We were eager to take turns looking through the lens at the stars above; the sky was reasonably dark and being a good distance away from city lights, we were able to view the celestial bodies rather clearly.

Allen, our resident scholar, began to explain to his young listeners the benefits of studying the stars.

"All the heavenly bodies were created by God," he began slowly. "He not only counted all the stars but he also called them by name. He placed lights in the firmament to divide the day from the night, and also for signs, seasons, days and years."

"Just imagine how boring life would be without the little daily changes we take for granted every day!" Chloe said interrupting. "I love watching the sun rise in the morning, but I love the sunsets just as much."

"And I love summer," Charlotte added, "but I long for winter when I see the leaves begin to fall."

"Autumn is my favorite time of year," I rejoined and a brief discussion ensued wherein each of our family members declared their particular seasonal favorite.

"Many scholars believe that man once knew all the names of the 'special stars' and that their knowledge of them was lost over time," Allen began again. "Job records evidence of several of them such as Arcturus, Orion and Pleiades. As a matter of fact, we will see if we can find Arcturus this evening," he added looking through the telescope.

"We enrolled Michael in a junior astronomy class taught by one of our friends," Victoria explained, "when we purchased the telescope. He's teaching the class from a biblical point of view."

Victoria then asked Michael if he could explain the difference between astronomy and astrology. He answered without hesitation.

"Astronomy is a science; it is the study of heavenly bodies. Astrology is a part of the occult that teaches the stars and planets are able to influence human affairs."

"Very good, Michael," Allen praised, "that's correct. The heavens actually declare the glory of God quite well. Astrology is a perversion of the truth; it's a counterfeit seeking to imitate the legitimate in an effort to deceive."

Allen's words brought to remembrance another counterfeit, a human one who had tried to usurp Christopher's position in the world. I shuddered when I recalled the events which transpired that eventually led to his death.

"Arcturus is a 'decan' star in the house of Bootes in the constellation of Virgo and its name means 'Watcher' or 'Guardian'; sometimes it means 'He cometh.'"

"If this star is in the constellation of Virgo, the Virgin, then is it supposed to be a representation of the Savior to come?" Edgar asked eagerly.

"Yes, it is from the Biblical perspective. All twelve constellations tell a story: the gospel written in the stars. In the constellation of Aries, the Ram, for example, you see the story of the Lamb that was slain.

"There are four principle symbols: Aries the Ram, Cassiopeia the Woman, Cetus the Sea Monster and Perseus the Warrior. Jesus Christ is depicted as the Ram, the lamb slain for the sins of mankind. The woman of course is the church, the bride of Christ. The Sea Monster is a picture of the devil who does all he can to deceive mankind; he desires their allegiance. And finally, Perseus, the Warrior King who walks on the brightest part of the Milky Way, symbolizes Christ as Conqueror. He is the one who breaks the chains that keep mankind in bondage to the devil and his lies.

"There is really so much more to learn but you need to study each constellation to see how the entire gospel story unfolds. It ends in the house of Leo the Lion in which, Regulus, one of its principal stars crushes the head of Hydra, the water snake, the devil.

"Allen, what book is your friend teaching from? I'd like to get a copy for my family to study together," Edgar asked.

"Me too," Scott and Devon echoed simultaneously. Allen responded with a promise to e-mail each a list, as there were several.

The family spent the rest of the evening leisurely stargazing; the night sky was magnificent. When bedtime rolled around, the children, exhausted from the long day outdoors, fell asleep quickly. The adults then spent some time alone talking over the events of the day.

"Allen," Scott began pensively, "I'm surrounded by religious skeptics all day long. You must be, at the university, too. Many of them believe in evolution and not creation; even if I could get them to listen to this interpretation of the stars, I don't think they'd accept it as valid. What do you say to them?"

"Well, when I approach people who come from an alternate belief system than my own, I try not to force feed them information they aren't interested in. If they are willing to listen, I try to open the door of their minds gradually. I never argue my point of view; I simply present it, pray, and allow the Holy Spirit to work."

"So many people, even those in the church, indulge in astrology because they believe it's harmless. They don't see anything wrong with just reading their horoscope," Devon added sadly.

"You're right and it's tragic that we don't know the Bible as well as we should, or that we compromise its teachings. Our home Bible study has been studying the book of Isaiah and many of our friends were startled to read what he wrote about astrologers, convicted as well. Let me get my Bible and I'll read it."

Allen walked into the house and came back minutes later carrying his large leather-bound Bible. He quickly found the passage he was referring to and read it out loud.

> *Stand now with thine enchantments, and with the multitude of thy sorceries…Thou art wearied in the multitude of thy counsels. Let now the astrologers, the stargazers, the monthly prognosticators, stand up, and save thee from these things that shall come upon thee. Behold, they shall be as stubble; the fire shall burn them; they shall not deliver themselves from the power of the flame…*[2]

"Pretty scary!" Devon said.

"Astrology is dangerous; we need to remember that!" Allen replied.

"I think it's time for something a little lighter," Charlotte said wisely. "Let's raid the kitchen and have a midnight snack." Everyone stood up and light chatter filled the air as we headed toward Martha's sanctum in search of refreshment. Allen and I were the last to leave the back yard.

---

[2] Isaiah 47: 12-14 KJV

"Allen," I asked quietly, "The Milky Way is a faint band of light crossing the entire sky. Does it have any special significance?"

"Yes," Allen affirmed softly. "Many believe it's there to remind us that the precious blood of Christ flows as a River of Life that encircles the globe."

"Amazing!" I replied.

Chapter Twenty-four

Dictionary Words

*O*n the whole most of the members of our family were early risers; even those who liked to sleep late had no problem getting up when a fun-filled event was planned for the day. Today, we were going to the beach again and the grandchildren were anxious to get an early start. They all had assigned chores to perform after breakfast, determined by their age and ability, and once they were completed they could go outdoors or play a game until we were ready to leave.

The older children spent a portion of their summer vacation working on their reading, writing and math. They were given a new list of dictionary words every week, assigned by their mothers, to enhance their vocabularies. When all of the children were together, their mothers created competitive games for them to play to boost their enthusiasm for study.

Victoria had compiled this week's list of assigned words and given them to Michael, Dari, E.J., Eliza and Riley; the words had to be defined first and then used in a story each child would write alone. The best overall story would receive a prize. It was a fairly resourceful way to encourage the children to continue their education over the long, hot summer.

At breakfast that morning "the big five" spoke about their latest creative efforts.

"I'm writing an adventure story," Michael began. He was also reading *Treasure Island*, a wonderful source of inspiration.

"I am too," Eliza echoed, a little miffed; she was reading *The Secret Garden.*

"You can both write adventure stories," Charlotte said in a soothing manner. "I'm sure your storylines will develop very differently." Her words seemed to settle Eliza's little ruffled feathers.

"I'm not telling what my story is about," E.J. insisted. He was currently reading *Chronicles of Narnia.*

Dari and Riley had yet to utter a word. I knew Dari was reading *Little Women*, and that Riley had taken *Tom Sawyer* out of the children's library upstairs where they often found their summer reading materials.

Charlotte created the children's library in the converted nursery on the third floor, which was currently being used as an indoor play room. She acted as head librarian and the children could "check out" any book they wanted for a period of one month. All of the "big five" were expected to read one new book every month from June to September to stimulate their imaginations; television was limited to one hour a day unless the family was watching something special together.

Chloe's Caitlin was too young to participate in most of the games, as was Ethan, so Chloe invested her time in teaching the two youngsters lessons appropriate to their age and ability. They were doing well working on learning to identify their A, B, Cs and numbers.

We were fortunate having so many teachers in the family, and it was an added blessing that they wanted to use a portion of their free summer time vacationing together. Even Dr. Devon took a month off from the hospital so Dari could be included in activities with her young cousins; she felt it was especially important for her fatherless daughter to spend time with her extended family.

This morning the grandchildren completed their chores in record time; once they were finished they met in the kitchen so

Martha and Mary could help them pack a picnic lunch for their day at the seashore. Allen, today's leader, herded the crowd of young-sters into the cars that would take them down to the beach. When the house was finally empty of their precious little souls, peaceful silence ensued.

One short business meeting kept me behind the group, but I would rejoin them later. Noah and I needed to discuss Sophie's replacement: an unanticipated dilemma.

I walked down the hill to the Tea Cottage and found Noah working out of his old tiny office. He had a spacious workplace located in our catalog center, which also included our industrial-sized kitchens; but he still spent a great deal of his time working at the Cottage. Perhaps because it was a silent source of inspiration.

When I walked through the large double doors I was greeted by the hostess on duty; it was Hannah Moore who was working here with her stepfather for the summer.

"Good morning, Mrs. Elliott," she said sweetly as I entered.

"Good morning, Hannah," I replied, "I have a meeting with your dad today."

"He's waiting for you," she said and then led me to one of the small booths in the converted stable where Noah was diligently reviewing some paperwork.

"Good morning, Rachel," Noah said standing up when I entered. "Hannah, please tell the server to bring those samples I set aside for Mrs. Elliott," he said and Hannah quietly obeyed.

We talked for a few moments until the server entered carrying a sample plate of new items the chefs had prepared for the fall menu. He left them on a side table as Noah directed.

"I think you'll like this pumpkin soup," Noah said, placing a small tureen in front of me. I took several spoonfuls and smiled with approval; it was truly delicious.

"Oh, this is wonderful, Noah," I said in agreement. There were three new sandwiches, tasty cobblers, sweet potato pie, and an assortment of seasonal truffles. We talked over the menu and some personnel changes that would occur once school resumed in the fall before we addressed the managerial position at the inn.

"I've received several exceptional resumes," Noah began, hand-ing me copies of those he had approved; there were four. I looked through the resumes noting that all the candidates were extremely qualified, with sterling recommendations.

"Is something wrong?" he asked when I didn't react to any of the applicants.

"Nothing's wrong, Noah. Their credentials seem impeccable but I'm not sure any of these ladies would fit in." Noah looked at me curiously. "How would you describe them personally?" I asked.

"Personally?" he inquired. "I'm not sure; I guess I would say they presented themselves as skilled professionals; perhaps a little tempermental."

"And temperamental people are unpredictable people," I replied with a smile. "And while I want someone who is skilled, I also want someone who works well with others. We are a family-type enterprise and our interpersonal relationships are important to ensure harmony. The resident manager of the inn needs to fit in and blend with the key elements of our organization if we are going to continue to thrive as we do. No one enjoys working with a 'prima donna' so I'd rather hire someone with a little less skill if they are also steady and kind."

Noah smiled and said, "I understand; I know the kind of person you want but she may be difficult to find. Out of those who have applied for the position, these four were the most qualified even if a little stuffy. Why don't we leave Sadie in place temporarily since she's almost trained and continue our search?"

"That's agreeable!" I said and rose to leave and then remembering another subject I wanted to discuss, I turned back to Noah once again.

"Sophie was in the process of doing some redecorating to the inn; I want to make some changes here in the cottage as well. I think we should begin with the loft upstairs; what do you think?"

This time it was Noah's turn to smile. "I was going to suggest it myself."

"Good! Why not put some of your ideas down on paper and then we can talk them over when Chris returns." Noah agreed, and saying good-bye, I left the building.

I walked back up the hill with Prudence following silently behind; I found my beach bag and hat and waited while Sam brought the car around front. When he pulled up, Prudence and I climbed in the back and slowly headed toward the beach to meet the children. In no time at all, I was dipping my feet in the cold salty water and scurrying in the sand with our youngsters.

Eventually I made my way over to the secluded area that the family had chosen to set up beach umbrellas and blankets; I picked a cold can of iced tea from the beverage cooler and sat down in a shady area. Lying back in the warm sand I eventually closed my eyes and relaxed.

Chapter Twenty-five

An Angelic Revelation

"Rachel," Riley called from the seashore, "please, come and play with me!"

My little brother always wanted me to play with him; couldn't he see I was busy building sand castles?

"Rachel, why don't you go and swim with your brother," my mother cajoled sweetly.

"Oh, mother," I sighed, "do I have to?"

"No," she replied, "but Riley is little and he feels safer being in the water with you."

"But he's with Daddy," I protested.

"But Daddy isn't as much fun as you are," she replied with a smile. My mother's face shone brightly in the sun; her long hair was the color of spun gold and I loved the way it hung down her back in loose ringlets. Riley favored her with his short curly golden locks. My hair was much more like my father's: thick and coarse and auburn.

"Oh, okay," I said feeling resentful. "Being the big sister isn't easy," I declared and mother only laughed; she was so tender even when I was gruff.

"Thank you, Rachel," she said as I headed down to the shore.

"Rachel, Rachel, Rachel," Riley cried, jumping up and down with joy. "Come on, I'll race you," he said, and laughing we jumped into the churning surf together. It really was wonderful although I wouldn't admit it out loud.

I took hold of Riley's small hand and we ventured into the waves; Daddy was watching us from the shore.

"Stand with your back to the waves, Riley," I commanded; being older and wiser did have its advantages. Riley always listened to me because he thought I was wonderful. "Hold on to me tightly, Riley, the water is going to pull us back…hold on…hold on tight!"

The water streamed past us pulling on our bodies and we struggled to stay standing. We laughed noisily as the surging waves were tremendously exhilarating.

"Hold on to me, Rachel; don't let go, don't let go!" Riley shouted in excitement and fear.

The waves were strong and powerful. "Let's move in a little closer to shore, Riley," I said, fearful the ocean's strength would overpower me.

"Just one more wave," Riley pleaded.

"Okay, but hold on tighter," I shouted and we laughed as the next wave approached.

"Hang on, Riley, hang on!" I yelled fearfully but the wave proved too strong and as it swept over us it pulled Riley down and under. I tried to cling to his hand but his fingers lost mine and in seconds Riley was gone.

"Riley," I screamed afraid my brother would drown, "Riley, where are you?" I shouted with fear. I looked all around but Riley was nowhere in sight. Where was Daddy?

"Daddy," I yelled in terror. "Daddy, Riley's gone under." Frantically, I dove deep into the water searching for my young brother. But the waters were now dark and murky and filled with a mass of seaweed.

Suddenly, my body was jerked downward by an underlying current; it sucked me into the deep briny waters and I struggled to break free; I needed air. I reached for the light above but I was powerless to ascend. My lungs felt as though they would burst and then the light disappeared and darkness enveloped my eyes. My body went limp and I began to float in the water; a feeling of peace swept over me and then magically a light appeared in the darkness. A voice called out to me saying, "Reach out your hand, Rachel," but I couldn't move no matter how hard I tried. Then I saw him standing over me, his large hand descended, and grabbing hold of my arm, he quickly plucked me from my watery grave. Sputtering mouthfuls of seawater I gasped for breath and quickly inhaled huge gulps of fresh air, coughing and choking as I did.

"Rachel, are you all right?" My father asked as I clung to his right arm.

"I was scared," I said shivering. "I was afraid Riley would drown," I cried out softly.

Riley, already situated in my father's left arm, gave me a hug.

"I'm okay, Rachel," he said warmly. "An angel pulled me out of the water," he explained. I looked at him in disbelief.

"Don't lie, Riley," I said now angered by my brother.

"I'm not lying, Rachel," he said looking hurt. "There was an angel in the water and he pulled me out and brought me over to Dad."

"Enough of angels, enough talk altogether," Daddy said carrying us to the shore where mother was anxiously waiting. "Let's get dried off and go back to the Castle."

Mama and Daddy took us back to my grandparents' home and sent us to our rooms for a nap before dinner. I lay on my bed unable to sleep. Riley must have been confused; he couldn't have seen an angel. I also felt remorse because I knew Riley never lied.

"Rachel," someone whispered at my door, "are you awake?" It was Riley; he opened the door a little and peered in.

"You're supposed to be napping, Riley. You better go and lie down or you might get in trouble," I warned, not ready to acknowledge my sin.

"But Rachel," my brother said sorrowfully, "I can't go to sleep if you're mad at me." Riley was at my bedside in seconds; his little face filled with sadness he knelt down beside me. Oh, how I was humbled by his tenderness and that hurt even worse.

"Riley, I'm sorry I called you a liar," I confessed, feeling ashamed. "You don't *really* believe you saw an angel, do you?" I asked unconvinced.

"I'm not telling a lie, Rachel; I promise I'm telling the truth. I saw an angel and he pulled me up and out of the water. My foot was tangled in the seaweed and he set me free. He saved me, Rachel. And you know what he told me?" He asked grinning with excitement. "He said he'd come back soon to take me to see Jesus."

I stared at my brother bewildered by his words; he couldn't be making this up.

"He told you he was going to take you to see Jesus?" I asked slowly.

"Yes, but Rachel, don't tell, okay?" Riley said wistfully. "It will make Mama sad." His cherubic little face looked deeply into mine and then he kissed my cheek. "I love you, Rachel," he said matter of factly. "Don't be sad when I'm gone."

I sat up in my bed and pulled my brother to my side and hugged him so tightly I was afraid he would break. "I love you, too, Riley. Always remember that I love you."

I never told Mama or Daddy what Riley had confided to me; the angel did come back the following summer to take Riley and Mama and Daddy went too. In a strange way Riley's admonition had prepared me for his death, only I didn't realize it at the time. That last year of Riley's life was good; we spent a great deal of time together and I worked to be worthy of being the big sister he admired. In doing so I also became his best friend.

"Mama," Charlotte called, "are you awake?" I opened my eyes and looked at my daughter. "I must have dozed off for a few minutes," I confessed with a laugh.

"We're getting ready to go back to the house now," she said. "Edgar and the guys promised the kids pizza tonight. Mary and Martha are going to a movie with a friend."

"That sounds great," I replied. "I love pizza."

We packed up our belongings and piled into our cars and drove home. After a shower and a change of clothes we went outdoors to play a few games while we waited for our pizza to be delivered.

I sighed when Allen set up the Trivial Pursuit game; the battle of the sexes was on once again as the men lined up against the ladies.

Charlotte asked to be excused from the game and volunteered

to play with the children; this gave Devon an opportunity to take her place without feeling left out because she was the only single female.

Ethan and Caitlin loved the swings so Charlotte and I took turns pushing them; it was wonderful listening to their squeals of delight as they called out, "Higher, Grandma, higher."

My mind drifted back to Riley who loved to swing as well. "Higher, Rachel, higher," he used to shout when we played together in our own backyard. A tear slipped down my cheek and I quickly brushed it away. I never knew if Riley's angelic revelation was real or just his vivid imagination; I only knew I was grateful that I had heeded the warning by showing my brother immeasurable love while he lived.

Chapter Twenty-six

Maggie Richardson

"*I* want plain cheese," Riley said to his mother as she served up generous slices of pizza to her sons. "I would like to have a piece of plain cheese pizza, please, Mother. Is that what you meant to say, Riley?"

"Yes, Mama," he replied quietly. "Please!"

"Okay, Darlin'," she answered as she kissed him on the head. "Please take a seat next to your Dad or Michael," she said and off he went, gingerly carrying his dinner. The patio was really lovely this evening and it was a fine night to be eating outdoors.

"Oh, there are too many choices!" I exclaimed as I examined the different pizzas the children had ordered.

"Mom, the barbecued chicken is delicious," Devon said gobbling down a slice.

"The Canadian bacon with pineapple is my favorite," Chloe declared.

"I want one with everything," Victoria said, eyeing the messy-looking pizza with gusto.

"Not me, no thank you!" I said, knowing it would be too much for my digestion.

159

"There's pepperoni and sausage and we also ordered a veggie delight," Charlotte said, pointing out the other possibilities.

"I think I'll try the chicken, thank you." I said taking a large slice.

Cold drinks and salads were on the serving counter just outside the French doors that opened out to the patio. I poured a glass of lemonade and served myself a bowl of salad and finding a vacant seat next to Devon and Dari I sat down; we then prayed over our food and began to eat.

"Who is winning the game so far?" I ventured to ask Devon while munching on my salad.

"The men are," she said with a frown, "but the evening is still young," she said with exuberance.

When dinner was over and the game resumed, Charlotte and I cleaned up the few dishes there were and took the little ones in for a bath. We then took turns reading them short stories before bed and once all were tucked in for the evening we joined the others on the patio for coffee and dessert.

The adults later retreated to the parlor to play a few games and when Martha and Mary returned home at ten they were thoroughly engrossed in a game of Monopoly, playing as quietly as possible since the children were asleep.

I had withdrawn to the study to enjoy a little reading, and I was thoroughly immersed in a gaslight mystery novel when Martha tapped on the open door.

"Come in," I said, seeing my friend's face. She looked quite solemn when she entered so I sat up immediately to address her. "Is something wrong?" I asked fearfully.

Martha sat down in a chair across from me to speak.

"No, Mum," she said right away. "But I want to talk with ya about my good friend, Maggie." Martha's Irish brogue was thick tonight, a sure sign of stress.

"Maggie Richardson?" I queried.

"Yes," she replied. "Ya know that her husband's been an Alzheimer's patient for years?" she asked, and I nodded that I did. "Well, he's come down with pneumonia and is in hospice care; she told us tonight that he's not expected to live much longer." Martha retrieved a handkerchief from her purse and wiped her eyes. "She's in pretty dire circumstances; she's sixty ya know and in need of a job. His medical expenses cleaned out their savings and she had to sell her house too and, now, she's all alone living in a tiny apartment she can barely afford."

"Has she ever worked? Does she have an occupation?" I asked with concern. It wouldn't be easy for her to find a position; many employers didn't want to hire people in their sixties.

"She was a loyal and faithful wife for forty years, Mum." Martha said proudly. "Never had any children and now she's about to be a widow. She has no one to care for her, but Maggie's a diligent worker and a very good cook," she quickly added, and coming from Martha no higher praise was possible.

"And you're thinking she could…" I said leaving the question dangling in the air.

"I think she could fill Sophie's position at the inn," she replied bluntly.

"Well, let me pray about it tonight and then talk to Noah tomorrow, Martha, and see what he thinks!" I said softly.

"Ah, thank ya, Mum. I knew if anyone would understand and come to her aid, it would be ya." Martha's eyes continued to tear but being the stoic she was, she quickly thanked me and walked out the door toward the kitchen.

"Maggie Richardson!" I said quietly. "Let's see what door God wants opened for you!" I returned to my book and read until eleven and then took Baby out for a short walk before going to bed.

The next morning after breakfast the children went into the parlor to play a game Charlotte had created called "Build a Story." She held their list of spelling words in her hand and assigned each child a word. Then she began a story with one sentence and going around the room each child had to add a sentence using their word while building the story.

"Let's begin," she said, giving the children notice they needed to quiet down before starting. "My word is *TREASURE*," she said and several of the children groaned. "I wanted that word Mama," E.J. said boldly. His mother looked sternly at him and he quickly said, "I'm sorry."

"While walking down the street one day," she began enthusiastically, "my eyes fell upon an open map laying face up with the words 'buried *TREASURE*' written in the center."

Charlotte finished and pointed to Eliza who was next.

"I picked up the map and put it in my pocket in case any PIRATES were around."

"When I looked at the map later I noticed it had a picture of a big golden SEA CHEST filled with enormous jewels drawn on top of a large X," Dari added at her turn.

"But what I really wanted was the bag of DOUBLOONS I saw sitting on top of the jewels," E.J. said with pleasure.

"The treasure was buried on a big ISLAND in the ocean," Riley said shyly.

"So I packed my bag and hopped aboard a magnificent SAIL-ING SHIP in search of my prize." Michael said pleasantly ending the story.

"Nice touch, Mike," Charlotte praised. "You all did exceptionally well and I'd like to add a little Scriptural comment: in the Bible it says, 'All who seek shall find.' And since today's topic has been buried treasure, you will find some treasure buried in the sandbox out back." Charlotte had barely dismissed the children when they raced outdoors to search for their rewards, which Patrick had hidden earlier in the morning.

"What a great game that is!" Chloe said. "I can't wait for Caitlin to be old enough to participate."

"Don't hurry her," I said with a smile. "Children grow up fast enough and then they're gone in the blink of an eye; so enjoy every moment you have!"

"Mom, we promised the kids we'd take them to see a movie in town today; do you want to go?"

"Oh, I'd love to but I don't think I can; I need to take care of some business for Martha. Thanks anyway, Devon." The girls went outside to be with their children while I made a few phone calls: the first was to Noah and the second to Maggie Richardson.

Noah's schedule was flexible so if Maggie was available I hoped to set up an interview with her right away. When I called her home she said she was just on her way out to visit her husband and asked if she could stop by later in the day. I agreed and we promised to meet at the Victorian at two o'clock.

Martha, Mary and Maggie had been friends for years; they were all originally from County Cork, Ireland and met through friends of friends of relatives back home, so to speak. Maggie had lived in Thousand Oaks, California, not far from where we lived in Lake Sherwood, where she cared for her retired husband as long as she could until his Alzheimer's worsened and he became uncontrollable. While she was preparing to sell her home and move, Martha and I relocated to my grandparents' estate. Maggie was fortunate to find a facility that could care for her husband near a distant cousin who was living in Shell Beach; so, after getting him settled, she moved into an apartment nearby. Unfortunately, her cousin died rather abruptly in an auto accident and she was left virtually alone. Since then Martha had been her only real source of comfort and support.

Sophie was now working four long days a week and spending weekends with her mother as planned. She had prepared the dining room of the inn for dessert and coffee at my request; I wanted our meeting with Maggie to be an informal affair. I asked Sophie to attend the interview because even though she was leaving her opinions still mattered.

Walking through the front door of the Victorian always brought pleasant memories to mind. Today, it was dressed up with bouquets of summer flowers that added to its warm and homey atmosphere, which we tried to maintain for our guests. Sophie's personal charisma reflected delicately in the peaceful surroundings in a variety of ways, just as Miriam's had when she managed the inn years before. The furnishings were almost the same but little changes to the décor, subtle as they were, made an interesting difference.

Maggie arrived promptly at two and accepted a cup of tea and lemon cookies Sophie had baked earlier in the day. Sophie's knowledge and expertise in the kitchen had increased as much as her poise and serenity, and I began to realize just how much she had grown into her current position. Perhaps the real reason God was moving her on was because her time with us had ended and she had new horizons to pursue. It wasn't easy for her to go and it wasn't easy for us to let her go, but it was necessary so she could continue to grow in strength and character.

We spent the better part of an hour talking to Maggie about the inn and the range of responsibilities she would have if she were accepted as its resident manager. Noah, not wanting to place an unnecessary burden on her, asked if she could return one day to give us a practical demonstration of her culinary abilities; in response she asked if she might see the kitchen and prepare something "off the cuff" right away. Since we weren't in a hurry, we agreed.

Forty-five minutes later we were presented with two different meals: light, fluffy buttermilk pancakes with homemade blueberry topping and an enormous veggie omelet covered with jack cheese, potatoes O'Brien and thick slices of crisp bacon. Her presentation was simple but pleasing to the eye and the food was cooked to perfection; Martha hadn't been wrong.

We ate and talked and even Sophie relaxed, joining in the conversation asking Maggie a bevy of questions about food preparation and favorite recipes. When Noah asked if she was able to use a computer and the Internet, Maggie confessed that she could navigate a little but that was all. "I'm willing to learn though," she added with a brave smile.

Sophie gave Maggie a quick tour of the Victorian and when the interview ended, we sent her home with a basket of goodies Noah had prepared from the Tea Cottage. I told her someone would call with a response within the week knowing in my heart the job was hers; only Noah needed to be convinced.

Chapter Twenty-seven

Discrimination

*T*he children returned from the movies exhilarated over the latest offering from Disney, which had both the boys and girls wishing they could be race car drivers. Oh, to be young again, I thought!

"Go outside and get some exercise," Victoria said to her two sons who were buzzing around the house like it was a racetrack.

"They need to burn off some energy," Charlotte said with a strained smile while directing her little ones outdoors.

"You could ask Patrick to take them for a walk in the orchards and let them pick fruit for a while," I suggested.

"That's a great idea, Mom!" Devon chirped. "I think practical hard work is good for everyone; I remember when we three girls used to pick fruit. It was fun."

"It was dirty you mean," Victoria said, wrinkling her nose to show her disdain.

"It's hard, honest work," I replied, "and it will help the children appreciate those who do that work for a living every day," I added strongly.

"Oh, no, Vic, Mom just gave you her 'raised eyebrow' look.

You're in deep trouble my dear!" she said laughing. Victoria only waved her off with a smirk.

"Come on," Devon said to Charlotte, "let's go with Patrick and the kids; it will be fun."

"Okay, I'm game. Chloe, do you want to join us?" Charlotte asked.

"I'd love to," she replied and they rounded up the children and headed them outdoors while I called Patrick.

"Patrick will be here in ten minutes," I told the girls who were waiting patiently on the patio with my overanxious grandchildren. When he finally arrived, he was carrying small burlap knapsacks we kept in the storage room. He gave one to each of the older children, and they eagerly carried them up the hill to the orchards behind the estate.

Victoria decided to remain behind and went into the study to watch the evening news while waiting for the men to return home from their sporting event. I got a cup of coffee from the kitchen and joined her.

"Another earthquake in Thailand; two hurricanes off the coast of Florida and a severe heat wave in the Midwest killing a number of people, mostly the elderly," she announced, "and that's what they reported in the first five minutes."

"What about the bombings in London? Do they have any new information about them? Has anyone been apprehended?" I asked, thankful that Christopher had missed the latest scourge plaguing England.

"No, not yet but I'm sure if there's any new information it will come in their detailed report later on. I'm just not sure I even want to watch anymore," she continued. "I know there isn't much we can do about the weather, but it scares me that so many people seem bent on evil. I'm really concerned about the future our children will face."

"I know their prospects don't look as bright as ours did when I was your age," I said, "but God is still in control. As bad as things get, nothing happens without his permission; we also need to realize that many of the things happening in the world are the result of his judgment for the wrongs we've committed."

"What terrible things did the people in your church do?" Victoria asked a little sarcastically. "Look at all the calamities that have befallen your congregation this year; and you strive to do so much good. It doesn't seem fair, does it?" she asked, truly upset.

"The sun shines on the just and the unjust," I proclaimed, "just look at righteous Job. We can't be angry at God when bad things happen; he always has a purpose for allowing us to suffer even when we don't know what it is. Our community has gone through a lot this year but we continue to press on; the school is in the process of being renovated and the church repairs are underway as well. Behind every cloud there's a rainbow; remember that!"

When Noah and I finally met again to discuss Maggie Richardson, his heart appeared a bit more open to her engagement, which was a relief.

"Noah," I began tactfully, "I know you have reservations about hiring Maggie because of her inexperience and age. She isn't computer savvy, and while I consider that to be a concern, I also know it's an easy obstacle to overcome. We can either have the office staff handle the inn reservations or we can ask Sadie to take over that aspect of the work." Noah agreed that either solution would work.

"You're right, Rachel. I'm not opposed to hiring Maggie but as your business manager it's my job to give you good business advice. The more qualified applicants weren't as personable as Maggie, I agree; she's very down to earth and likable. They had impeccable credentials but she more than demonstrated that she's capable in the kitchen even if less artistic. She also proved that she could be industrious and improvisational, a definite plus. I do believe she'll fit in well. What I'm most concerned about, however, is her age."

"Are you biased, Noah?" I asked surprised.

"You think I'm biased because of her age?" he asked, shocked.

"Are you?" I asked softly. "Aren't we all a little predisposed to buy into the cultural tendency that 'new is better than used' and 'young is better than old'? Isn't that what we call discrimination?"

"I'm not trying to discriminate against her, Rachel."

"Of course you aren't," I replied staunchly, "not consciously anyway. You simply want to hire the best person possible for the position and that will always be a matter of opinion. But let me tell you why I believe Maggie may be that person.

"Maggie's been faithful to her husband for forty years regardless of how difficult that has been. She's sacrificed her home, her life and basically her retirement to care for him. She's entering the work force at the age of sixty and that isn't easy; she's willing to learn and she isn't afraid of hard work. She's mature and apparently reliable according to the personal references she supplied, which you verified. She also comes with the highest recommendation possible: Martha believes in her.

"Now even though I don't know Maggie well, I know Martha extremely well. She has been a faithful friend and loyal employee for more than thirty years; and in my opinion anyone she recommends at least deserves a chance.

"You and I have known each other for some years, Noah. You are like a son to me; I admire you and respect your opinion. As far as the hiring goes I usually give you a free hand, except in key positions like this one. I want the people who work directly for me to feel like family; and I want them all to get along well. I'd like to help Maggie Richardson succeed. What do you say?"

Noah smiled his beautiful dimpled smile.

"Rachel," he said heartily, "if Maggie is your choice I will do everything I can to help her be successful. Since she isn't computer savvy, I think we need to hand those responsibilities over to Sadie as we discussed, at least while Maggie is in training.

"Hector Guirmo, who I hired last month when he graduated from the U.C.S.B., is working out well. He's already taken over some of Sadie's work and if necessary I can transfer the rest of her responsibilities to him in order to allow her to work full-time with Maggie until she gets established at the inn, which will also benefit Sophie."

"Sounds like a good plan, Noah. I meant to ask you how he was doing. He speaks several languages, doesn't he?"

"Yes, he has to extend his visa in order to remain here to work but I don't believe that will be a problem. He has unimpeachable credentials and passed our very stringent security check with flying colors."

"Thank you, Noah," I said when we completed our business. "Thank you for understanding."

"Well, I was in the same position when I started here, wasn't I?" he asked sweetly. "You opened doors for me too, Rachel."

Chapter Twenty-eight

Daddy's Day Out

Martha cried tears of joy when I told her Maggie Richardson was going to be the new resident manager of the inn, at least temporarily; she would be on probation for ninety days just like any other employee but we promised to do all we could to help her succeed.

Daddy's Day Out was a monthly event all the children enjoyed with their respective fathers, including Dari who received the attention of a surrogate. Under normal circumstances it was Christopher, Scott or Edgar but this month Noah had volunteered to act as her substitute parent to participate in the fun with the rest of the family.

This month's event was an excursion to the park where the men and their children could roller skate and then go out to lunch; fast food was always a big treat allowed only during these special paternal activities. Under normal circumstances they were, as Papa would say, *verboten*.

The July weather had been cooler than normal and the day being especially lovely we ladies decided to spend it outdoors as well. So, while the grandchildren were away with their fathers, we enjoyed a late morning meal in the Tea Cottage gazebo gardens, which had been created in an old horse paddock below the converted stables.

The air was fragrantly filled with the aroma of flowers now abounding with colorful blossoms. One of my favorite rose trees flourished with large perfect buds. Those that were open were luminously brilliant; the petals had bright yellow centers that flared into a fiery orange-red color on the tips. They were so vibrant they looked like they were on fire!

The gardens had seasoned over the years and taken on an idyllic character; the quaint cobblestone foundation gracefully upheld the tall white colonnades now pulsating with summer foliage in numerous shades of green. The hanging fuchsias were resplendently robed in bright pink, red and purple flowers and added to the leisurely charm of the al fresco décor. The tables were covered with pink tablecloths and napkins and adorned with tall vases filled with the flower of the week, which were white lilies.

Miriam, who was working at the inn for a few days so Sophie could spend more time with her mother, was on the premises so we invited her to join us. Hannah was on duty working and was delighted to be our server.

The tables in the garden were relatively small as they were designed for intimate settings, but we had an area reserved for large parties where tables could be joined together. We found our section and chose our seats with a great deal of animation and delight. The view of the ocean was spectacular from where we were seated and while we waited for Hannah to pass out menus, we watched people swimming and playing on the beach just as we had days earlier.

"What would you like to drink today, Aunt Rachel?" Hannah asked, ready to take our beverage order.

"I think I'd like a hot cup of berry tea," I said thoughtfully, "it's my favorite!"

"Oh, that sounds good," Miriam added quickly. "I'll have that too, Sweetie!"

"Okay, Mom," Hannah said with a smile.

Charlotte ordered a soda, Victoria and Devon both had raspberry iced tea and Chloe asked for a lemonade. While Hannah went to fill our order we talked as we surveyed the lunch menu.

"The turkey sandwich with spouts on grilled sourdough looks delicious," Charlotte said and Victoria agreed wholeheartedly.

When Hannah returned she told us about the soups of the day.

"We have fish chowder, chicken rice or vegetable barley soup if you want something hot; we also have cold peach soup topped with fresh cream and a sprig of mint.

"The chef's lunch special today is a smoked chicken and walnut salad on a croissant served with a fruit boat and yogurt dressing." Miriam and I both opted for the lunch special, which sounded delicious; Devon decided on the fish chowder and sourdough toast, Victoria and Charlotte ordered the turkey and Chloe ordered the peach soup and a croissant. Hannah quickly wrote down our order and headed off to the kitchen.

"I wonder how the boys are doing with the children," Victoria said with a sly smile.

"Scott is wonderful with Caitlin," Chloe began, "but she is little and she can be a handful when she's tired." Her face mirrored her anxiety.

"It's good for her to be with her father," Victoria responded. "Men parent differently than women do so it's good for kids to spend time with their fathers since most are in the care of their mothers on a regular basis."

"And when they come home they appreciate us all the more," Charlotte added with a smile.

"I know how important these little excursions are for Dari," Devon confided to the group, "especially because there's no man in our home anymore. She loved spending time with Joseph when he was alive; I know she misses him a lot. Bedtime is the worst because he always told her such wonderful stories."

"Yes, Joseph was a great storyteller," Charlotte said. "The children still talk about his fish story whenever they get out the fishing rods he gave them."

"Joseph's death was a terrible tragedy," Victoria began, "and I'm sorry you're alone, Devon, but you're doing a really great job raising Dari; I know it isn't easy for you."

"No, it isn't, but then I feel really fortunate to have such a supportive family to help me; so many women today are raising children on their own with no help from anyone. It's hard to work and be a mother and father to a child; and I have a great job and Mary besides."

I listened as my daughters shared their thoughts and feelings with each other and I heaved a sigh of gratitude that we were all together. It hadn't been easy for any of us when Paul left; Devon took it harder than the rest and for a period of time our family was in shambles. But the Lord had redeemed our lives and given us a good future together; He had brought all the children back close to our home borders and I was infinitely thankful.

It didn't take long before Hannah reappeared first with our beverage order and then with our meal; she served us with efficiency and ease.

"Thank you so much, Hannah," Chloe said upon receiving her lunch. "You make everything look so easy; I imagine you've had a wonderful teacher." Miriam smiled when Chloe looked in her direction. She was definitely pleased.

"Well, I've been here since I was ten," Hannah began, "and yes, I have had a wonderful teacher; my mother is not only a fantastic cook she's also a great example for me."

"What a generous compliment, Hannah," Miriam said with pride. "Thank you."

"How old were you when you came to the inn, Hannah?" Chloe asked again.

"Actually, I was ten and a half; although my mother frequently told people I was only *nine*."

"Did I?" Miriam asked with a quizzical smile.

"You did!" Hannah responded teasingly.

I smiled but remained silent. Hannah and I both knew why Miriam often miscalculated her age in those days; the last year with her husband, Hannah's father, had been so terrible she had blotted out portions of time from her mind. Those days were now over thankfully; God had redeemed their lives as well.

Chapter Twenty-nine

Wailing Women

*T*he luncheon proved sweet and refreshing and while the food was delectable the fellowship was immeasurably better. We returned home feeling vibrantly refreshed and ready for our family who arrived shortly thereafter. There were several skinned knees to patch and very dirty clothes to be changed but all in all their day together had happened as expected without any major mishap.

In the afternoon mail I received a brief note from Chris, who was currently corresponding only by post. He said he was well and that he and Wesley would be home soon and not to worry; the details about his arrival would follow. I called Vianca to share the brief bit of information I had received and promised to contact her if anything further arrived. She in turn said she had received a note from Wesley basically providing her with the same bit of news.

Myra called late in the afternoon the following day to finalize a few details about our women's conference; the construction going on at the church and school made it impossible to host our event at either facility and since we wanted it to be close to town, we decided to have it at the ranch.

When the details of the conference were set, we spoke again of world events; I listened intently as Myra talked about the famine in Africa and the expulsion of Israelis from their homes in the Gaza Strip.

"You know what wailing women are, don't you, Rachel?" Myra asked solemnly.

"Of course," I replied, somewhat diverted. "They are women hired to mourn at funerals."

"Yes, they're called by the living to lament the dead and sometimes those about to die," she said rather cryptically. "The prophet Jeremiah told us that the world would perish and be burned up, becoming like a wilderness. And do you know why?"

"It must be God's judgment," I replied, listening more attentively than ever.

"You're right. Actually, Jeremiah said only wise men would understand what was happening. He went on to explain that God's reason for judgment was because the people had forsaken his law; they don't listen and they don't obey."

"So, the things happening upon the earth—the floods, hurricanes, earthquakes, drought, famine and disease—you believe all these things are directly related to the fact that men have forsaken the laws of God?" I asked, already knowing the answer.

"Yes, I do," she said with a sigh. "Don't you?"

"Yes, I'm afraid I do."

"We are living in a quagmire of moral decay! Call for the wailing women!" Myra said emphatically. When she grew silent I remained silent as well, giving her time to compose herself and her thoughts. "We are living in miry clay," she said and in a tone of disgust she added, "And many of us truly like it."

"Isn't that because too much of the salt has lost its flavor?" I asked, speaking of the believing church. "And when the salt loses its flavor it becomes good for nothing and must be thrown away. Just the point John Edwards was recently making to our church. He said many of us have grown lukewarm and indifferent to the world dying around us," I explained, "and we must change."

"We need to get back to basics, Rachel by honoring God's laws; we should have them written on our hearts," she said wistfully. "If people would only realize they were given for our own good because

God loves us. I know this may sound strange, but I believe that the disasters occurring around the globe are messages of love. God is trying to get our attention; he wants us to repent and turn away from sin before it's too late. Those who heed his warning will be saved and those who don't will, in time, reap his wrath."

A shiver ran up my spine at the enormity of what she was saying.

"I'm afraid most people won't look at these occurrences as warnings from God; too many believe that a God of love doesn't punish people," I quickly replied.

"It isn't punishment, it's chastisement. All good parents chastise their children for doing things that are harmful or potentially fatal; why would God do less?"

My conversation with Myra drew to an end on that note, and after saying good-bye, I quietly hung up the telephone and relaxed in my chair to ponder her remarks.

"Mrs. Elliott," Prudence said from the doorway, "a telegram has been delivered for you," she continued when I looked in her direction. She entered the room and handed me the missive and after I thanked her she departed.

I opened the envelope and removed the note inside. It said:
THURSDAY MIDNIGHT SB.

It wasn't signed but I knew it was from Christopher telling me he would arrive at Santa Barbara Airport on Thursday at midnight. He was coming home under the cover of darkness, and I wanted to know why.

Vianca was eager to see Wesley so I invited her to join us at the estate for the weekend so we could go to the airport together; she thankfully agreed and said she'd drive up early Thursday afternoon.

Charlotte arranged to have Avril, a young nanny, come on Thursday evening to care for the children so the adults could go out to dinner and a movie; Ruth, her colleague, came with her. The children, having been cared for by Avril on several occasions, were looking forward to her visit. She and Ruth arrived promptly at six o'clock and squeals of delight rang out when they entered the front door.

"*Bonjour, mes enfants*," Avril said in a lighthearted way.

"*Bonjour, Avril*," Michael replied clearly. Victoria had been helping him with his French pronunciation and Avril was clearly happy with his success.

"*Bongoor, Avril,*" the younger children exclaimed at varying times causing a rather discordant sound to fill the air but Avril was pleased by their attention and after hugging each child she introduced them all to Ruth, her friend.

"Dinner is ready," Martha announced and the two nannies escorted their young charges to the dining room for their meal. Charlotte and her sisters followed, and after leaving their instructions with the nannies, they and their husbands departed.

Vianca, who arrived at four o'clock, had unpacked and was enjoying a cold glass of lemonade when the dinner bell sounded. She joined me in the dining room with the grandchildren where we feasted on pot roast, carrots and potatoes and delicious brown gravy and dumplings.

"I want to leave a little early for the airport," I explained after we finished eating, "as I'm not sure what airline Chris and Wesley are coming in on. Chris flew from here to San Francisco and then to London when he left, but he may be returning through Los Angeles, I just don't know."

"I checked the flight arrivals before I left the office today," Vianca began, "and found a flight on United Airlines coming in from San Francisco at 11:53 P.M. It may be the one they're on," she said hopefully.

"Sounds logical; we'll check that one out first," I responded. "Better dress warm and comfortably," I suggested. "We may be there for awhile."

We left the house at nine with Sam and Prudence, who sat together in the front seat of the Suburban; Vianca and I were seated in the middle and there was plenty of room for Chris and Wesley. Not having spoken to either of them, we had no idea whether they would be traveling alone or with companions.

Sam parked the car in the short-term parking lot and together the four of us entered the airport terminal. We stopped at one of the concession stands and bought a cup of coffee and then made our way to the United Airlines gate to wait for the plane from San Francisco to arrive; it was precisely on time.

We watched from a window as the passengers disembarked in

the dark; it was difficult to see the faces of the occupants until they entered the terminal. At last, I spied Wesley as he walked through the door and saw Chris following close behind. I was surprised to see Gabe Shomer directly next to him and looking around quickly I realized Ralph, his twin brother had been in the lead. Wearing a hat pulled low over his forehead he was fairly indistinguishable.

"Chris," I called and my husband turned to look in my direction; seeing my face, he smiled. He and Wesley made their way through the crowd with the Shomer twins hovering over them.

"Rachel," my beloved said when we met, "I've missed you so much," and he leaned over and picked me up to give me a kiss.

"We shouldn't linger," Ralph said cautiously and Chris nodded. Gabe took the lead as we walked to the baggage area to recover their luggage and then we headed toward the exit.

Sam went ahead of us to retrieve the car and we waited inside the terminal until he arrived. When he pulled up outside, we left the building; Vianca and I quickly stepped into the rear seat of the Suburban with Prudence. Wesley opened the front door to sit next to Sam; Ralph stood outside the car behind the driver's door keeping watch while Chris climbed into the middle seat of the middle section with Gabe following behind. It seemed confusing but I had learned from experience not to question my security team; I just obeyed their instructions. It was obvious the twins wanted Chris between the two of them; I just wasn't sure why.

"Just a moment sir," someone called out and Gabe stepped back from the car and turned to see who it was. I bent down as well to try to see who had spoken and noticed a security guard approaching our vehicle; as he did, Gabe turned placing his hand on his holster. Moments later, I saw a car approach; it passed us and pulled ahead of our vehicle and stopped: then shots rang out. One, two, three, four, five, six…there were too many to count amidst a current of screams coming from a variety of people.

"NO, GOD, OH NO," I shouted. Prudence threw herself over my body and pushed me down into the seat. She grabbed Vianca, who was wailing and crying, and pulled her head down as well; I cried and prayed for mercy.

"Pull ahead, Sam," Prudence shouted her gun in her hand.

"I can't," he replied in anger, "we're boxed in."

I heard gunfire coming from several locations but didn't dare raise my head to see what was happening. Prudence managed to open the rear door of the car and was outside in an instant, pistol drawn ready for action.

Sirens blared loudly in the background, acting as momentum for the vehicle that had pulled alongside of us to disappear quickly into the darkness. It was all over in minutes; Ralph and Gabe quickly surveyed the situation and called for an ambulance.

The security guard was lying on the pavement; Gabe shot him but not before he managed to discharge several shots. Ralph had a gunshot wound to his left arm, which was bleeding but didn't appear serious.

"Wesley's hurt," Sam said to Gabe. "It's serious, too, I'm afraid." Vianca cried louder than ever but neither of us moved out of our seats.

"Christopher," I called quietly before leaning forward to speak to my husband but he didn't answer. "Chris," I shouted again and receiving no answer I sat up and reached for him.

Gabe leaned into the vehicle and took hold of Chris's shoulder; he was unconscious.

"He's been shot," he replied. "Looks bad!" he said as I began to cry.

The airport police arrived quickly along with an ambulance. Noise filled the evening air; people were talking, crying and shouting orders until it became almost deafening. Gabe addressed the authorities telling them who we were and what had transpired. Chris, severely wounded, was rushed to the hospital along with Ralph. Prudence and Sam hovered next to me and Vianca, who was crying hysterically. Gabe quickly joined us and directed us toward a police cruiser that whisked the four of us away to the hospital just as the coroner's van pulled up to retrieve the body of the counterfeit security guard, now lying dead on the pavement along with our dear friend Wesley.

Chapter Thirty

Casualties of War

Goleta Valley Cottage Hospital was only a few short miles from the airport; Vianca, still sobbing uncontrollably when we arrived, was eventually given a sedative to calm her nerves. Ralph's injury wasn't life threatening and after his flesh wound was treated he was released.

Christopher was rushed into surgery bleeding profusely; we found out later that he had a bullet in the left upper quadrant of his abdomen beneath the left rib cage. A bullet had also grazed his forehead but the wound wasn't deep and would only require a few stitches.

We were allowed to wait in a small private room where police and detectives could take our statements and conduct their initial interviews regarding the incident while we waited for news of Chris's condition.

I hesitated to call home, not knowing anything concrete about his medical status, but I knew Chloe needed to be informed about her father's situation. Victoria answered the telephone and I quickly explained to her what had happened before speaking to Chloe, who said she and Scott would leave immediately. I then spoke briefly to Devon, who agreed to accompany them to the hospital along with Patrick, who would bring Vianca back to the estate where she could rest.

It was a long night; the doctors eventually emerged from surgery but the news wasn't good. Christopher had been shot in the spleen and had lost a great deal of blood; a splenectomy was performed to remove it. Additionally, the small intestine had been perforated, which the doctor said could lead to a nasty infection called peritonitis.

"He is in good physical condition," the surgeon said quietly, "which is always beneficial. The spleen is a vascular organ that stores a great deal of blood; many people never make it into surgery because they die from blood loss. Fortunately, the airport is in such close proximity to the hospital that he was able to receive treatment immediately. Now, all we can do is wait; as I said, our greatest concern is infection."

Devon asked a few questions and then we thanked the doctor, who agreed to prepare a written statement to issue to the press. A hospital spokesman had been assigned to work with us to handle inquiries, which were already pouring in from numerous agencies. Devon and Scott had agreed to speak for the family if and when it became necessary.

Chris was in the ICU where we were able to visit him briefly. His head was bandaged and his face was a little swollen and discolored from his wound. He was extremely pale from the loss of blood but he was alive.

Chloe, Scott, Devon and I remained at the hospital all day on Friday; Charlotte and Edgar joined us in the morning for a visit and Victoria and Allen came later in the afternoon with a suitcase of clothing Martha had packed for me.

On Saturday morning Chloe and Scott returned to the estate to spend some time with Caitlin and promised to return later in the day. Victoria and Prudence worked together to secure several rooms at a nearby hotel for me and members of the family to use while Chris remained hospitalized.

Security was tighter than ever before and I knew Ralph and Gabe were communicating with their superiors at Interpol regarding what they considered to be an attempted assassination. While I rested in a chair in the ICU waiting room, I ruminated over a conversation I had with Gabe when we were alone. I had asked him if the events that transpired in Denmark could have provoked the attack on Chris's life. He calmly apologized for not being able to divulge any details regarding their trip, which I found increasingly frustrating, but when he added, "We are all potential casualties of war!" I was more perplexed than ever.

"Mom," Devon said softly to awaken me from my meditation.

"Is something wrong?" I quickly asked, seeing the worried look on her face.

"Chris has a high fever," she replied. "He's shaky and still unconscious; his blood culture came back negative for sepsis but because he's on antibiotics that could be a false reading. Wound infection is often a serious complication of surgery but the doctor is treating him with intravenous antibiotic therapy and he's receiving supportive therapy with oxygen, which should increase his blood pressure. Chris suffered the trauma of the gunshot wound, the loss of blood and then the surgery; his body is strong but it's been through a great deal."

There were tears in her eyes as she spoke and I sensed she was sharing the scientific truths she dealt with every day as lovingly as possible; she didn't want to hurt me but she knew better than I that Chris could die and she wanted me to be prepared.

I quietly walked into the ICU and stood next to his bed; he was restless, his skin was warm and he was very pale. I took hold of his hand and spoke softly into his ear the words of the Twenty-third Psalm and he seemed to relax a bit. I prayed it would somehow comfort him but in reality it was I who needed the comfort; and I turned to it now as I often did when faced with fearful thoughts and emotions.

Casualties of war; my mind wandered back to my conversation with Gabe.

"Chris isn't a soldier," I had replied sharply to Gabe without meaning to.

"We're all soldiers, Rachel," Gabe responded politely. "We're either members in the Army of God or we're members in the Army of Satan; battles are won and battles are lost as the war rages on.

Good men must fight and good men will die in whatever arena of conflict God chooses to use them; only the outcome is assured and we can live with hope knowing the victory belongs to the Lord."

I wept softly watching my husband struggle for his life knowing a battle was being fought inside his body. Would death conquer Chris? Or would he triumph over it and return to me?

Through my tears I prayed softly, "Though I walk through the valley of the shadow of death, I will fear no evil: for thou art with me;"[3]

---

[3] Psalm 23:4 KJV

Chapter Thirty-one

A Brief Respite

Devon, extremely practical in stressful situations, suggested we donate blood to replenish the supply for others who might need it. Christopher, whose blood type was AB positive, had needed a transfusion to replace the blood he had lost. And being extremely thankful to those anonymous individuals who had willing donated their blood to save lives we wanted to do the same. It was a welcome diversion that helped ease the stress of the long hours while we waited with hope and prayed for healing. So, when visitors came to the hospital to visit we asked those who could to donate blood.

As knowledge of Chris's injury reverberated around the globe, satellite trucks began to appear in the parking lot while reporters and photographers gathered in large numbers outside the hospital seeking answers to their questions regarding his "accident," the term now being used by the authorities.

Scott, who was a reporter for a cable news station, wrote a brief report for his agency, giving only pertinent information. The official statement released by the hospital originated through British Intelligence; their position was that the attack was simply a case of mistaken identity. Speculation as to the genuine cause of the attack was, however, as rampant as the misinformation now appearing in the media and on the Internet.

Late in the afternoon on Saturday, while Chris was sleeping peacefully, I was brave enough to venture outdoors to go to the hotel for a shower and some rest. Bombarded by reporters, I refused to comment on Chris's injuries, and protected by my entourage we made a hasty escape.

Hot water beat down upon my tired body relaxing my aching muscles. I climbed into a terrycloth robe and lying down upon the bed I easily fell asleep. It was dark when I awoke; my hair was wet and tangled but I quickly brushed it out, secured it with a clip and dressed so I could return to my husband's bedside.

"Any news?" I asked Prudence automatically while I dressed.

"No, nothing," she replied solemnly, "except that there are reporters outside the hotel and that concerns me."

Ralph had driven Prudence and me to the hotel and Sam had been left at the hospital to watch over the family; Gabe was near Chris at all times. Braving the sea of reporters at the hotel wasn't too difficult but when we arrived at the hospital they converged upon us like a swarm of locusts. My eyes were dazed by the constant camera flash from photographers taking my picture; and one reporter accidentally hit me in the jaw when he thrust his microphone into my face while asking a question. Ralph pushed him away as Prudence guided me through the hospital door.

"Are you all right, Mrs. Elliott?" she asked, concerned.

"I'm fine, Prudence, thank you," I replied as I walked toward the ICU.

I spoke with Chris's doctor shortly after my return only to hear nothing had changed. I thanked him for taking time to speak to the press and asked him to continue giving them daily updates; he agreed. Devon and Scott accompanied him to answer more personal questions regarding the family.

Saturday evening was long and tiring; Chris's condition was up and down all night long and I struggled to remain optimistic. I kept thinking about the possibility of sepsis; I knew Pope John Paul II had developed the illness after suffering from a urinary tract infection; the only difference was his poor health was probably the reason.

I was greatly surprised when Vianca walked into the waiting room with Charlotte and Edgar. "I can't just sit and feel sorry for myself," she began, giving me a warm hug. "Wesley wouldn't want me to." She took my hand and together we drew comfort from one another.

The early hours of the morning were the worst; I was tired but couldn't sleep. I just kept vigil by Christopher's side and waited for a response. Three, four, five o'clock passed with no change. Then, at about six o'clock sharp, he moved a bit and then groaned. My eyes focused on his face; it had a little more color. My hands touched his skin; it was slightly cooler.

He groaned again and then slowly he opened his eyes.

"Rachel," he whispered softly.

"Yes, Darling," I responded as tears slid down my cheeks.

"I love you," he said with a smile.

"I love you, too," I answered and tenderly kissed his lips.

Chapter Thirty-two

A Hellish Nightmare

Christopher's health fluctuated over the course of the next ten days but once he regained consciousness Sunday morning he steadily improved; he remained in the hospital a few days longer than were absolutely necessary but his doctor wanted to be sure he wouldn't suffer a relapse. We never spoke of Denmark during his long confinement as privacy was essential in discussions that dealt with international interests. And while I was anxious to have my questions answered I knew patience was a painful necessity.

Seven or eight days after his surgery Chris felt he was finally getting better; he was still extremely tired and in pain but he began to look and feel more like his normal self. Still, it wasn't until we were able to move him home that he began to share some of his feelings. Slowly, he divulged the very frightening fears he had been wrestling with inside.

"Have you ever thought much about hell?" he asked me abruptly one afternoon while we were eating lunch alone in our sitting room upstairs.

"Yes," I said carefully unsure of what had prompted the question. "Papa used to speak of it about as often as John Edwards does. Hell isn't something most people want to think about," I added and then asked, "Why?"

"Well, when I was unconscious I had this terribly perplexing dream," he began. "It must have been a nightmare but it felt strangely real and horribly bizarre, more bizarre than anything I've ever seen, heard or felt," he said vehemently. "What some might call Kafkaesque," he concluded with an odd sigh.

"Tell me about it," I said, sitting forward in my chair, frightened by the look on his face.

"I don't know if I can remember all of it," he said, rubbing his head where the bullet had grazed the skin; the wound was still red and swollen but it was healing. Christopher closed his eyes momentarily as if trying to recall the dream, and as he did, perspiration began to form on his skin.

"The first thing I remember is that I was falling," he began again. "Or at least I thought that I was falling because I was descending downward quite rapidly. At some point I realized that I wasn't falling, I was simply drifting peacefully downward. It was utterly dark all around me; the only light I perceived came from an object below; I couldn't tell what it was at first but as I drew closer I realized that the light was emanating from a city. The closer I came to it the more I was able to distinguish and by the time I had almost reached bottom I realized that there were actually two cities, one light and one dark, separated by a great river, which was completely engulfed in fire." Chris stopped and took a sip of water and then wiped his brow before continuing.

"My body automatically floated to the city of light on the right side of the river; it was breathtaking. A lovely green garden with fruitful trees and fragrant flowers surrounded a blue lake of crystal clear water; it was a tropical paradise of some sort but it was completely empty. I called out but no one answered; it appeared I was alone."

"Curious," I said, listening carefully but not wanting to interrupt him.

"I walked toward the edge of the garden to see if I could look below at the river of fire but an invisible force kept me from proceeding. So, instead, I glanced across the river toward the dark city on the other side; it too appeared empty. But I remember feeling utterly repulsed by the dim and dingy land, which was covered with some sort of loathsome gray moss.

"Mystified by my surroundings I glanced upward and was shocked by what my eyes beheld; there were people everywhere. I could see them clearly because they were walking on streets made of crystal. Men and women, young and old, were walking to and fro, carrying on their busy lives oblivious to what was happening down below. I shouted several times in attempt to draw their attention but they remained entirely unaware of my existence.

"I was now more perplexed than ever so I sat down to contemplate my situation. *How did I get here?* was my first thought but I simply couldn't remember. Looking above for the answer, I searched and searched until my eyes finally rested upon two obscure openings in the crystal ceiling. I surveyed them for some time until I realized they were actually portals into the city below; one was very wide and the other was extremely narrow.

"I was gazing intently at the two different openings, wondering why they were so vastly different, when an old man suddenly approached the narrow portal. Just as he was about to walk through, a man in white stepped forward; he appeared to be a door-keeper. He must have recognized the man seeking admittance because he quickly stepped aside so the man could step through the portal. He floated downward just as I had done earlier but when he arrived in the garden paradise, two men, also dressed in white, appeared and quickly whisked him away. In less than a second they were gone.

"Only moments later, I heard the sound of wailing coming from above and so I looked up; a second man was falling but he had come through the wide, open portal. He was descending rapidly but he wasn't floating, and he fell with a loud thud into the loathsome gray moss covering the dark city. As soon as he touched the ground it began to move; despicable beings arose from what I then recognized as decaying ashes; burning fire engulfed them, and taking hold of the man, who was by this time screaming and writhing in agony and pain, they pulled him downward after them. The city then returned to its previous character of dingy darkness, only now I knew its secret.

"This same scenario happened over and over and over again. And regardless of how many times I shouted a warning to those above walking near the broad portal, they continued to fall to their misery and doom in the dreaded city below."

"Hell does have a wide, gaping and open mouth," I said reflecting upon Chris's dream. "And there's nothing between men and hell except Jesus Christ; and he's there for all who are willing to turn to him," I said by way of rationalization.

"Your dream has elements of fear and warning; you fear for the lost and you're trying to intercede on their behalf. You see their fate clearly; you want to save them from it but you know people often don't listen until it's too late," I added perceptively.

"That's too true," he replied sadly.

"Papa used to say that when God speaks through dreams and visions he also provides the interpretation."

"Well, one thought keeps coming to mind whenever I think of my dream," Chris said mystically.

"And that is…" I asked, waiting for his response.

"That we all need a doorkeeper," he replied.

"Interesting," I said with a smile. "Very interesting!"

Chapter Thirty-three

Debriefing

Wesley's murder and Chris's injuries had brought our summer vacation to a rather abrupt end; and since the essence of the attempted assassination was yet unknown, the grandchildren were forced to spend their last week at the estate playing on the grounds as a safety precaution. There were too many questions that needed to be answered before we would truly know who was at risk and who wasn't and why.

When Victoria, Charlotte and Chloe left with their families, Devon remained behind an extra few days to make sure Chris would be all right; she was a joyful presence to those in need and I was sorry when she and her family returned home as well.

Chris, normally an early riser, slept late most mornings during his convalescence, disrupting our regular prayer time. So, while he slept I prayed alone in our little chapel; I had much to be grateful for beyond the miracle of his glorious resurrection. I was also thankful that he hadn't been permanently disfigured or disabled. As a matter of fact, I felt his injury almost inspired him with new purpose; it was as though God had brought him back for a specific reason.

I was sitting quietly in the chapel almost finished with my morning mediations when the door opened and he walked in. I stood up and walked over to greet him.

"Good morning, Sleepy Head," I said, giving him a kiss.

"Good morning, Darling," he replied with a smile.

"What's up? You look so serious," I said, a little worried.

"Rachel," he began, "I think it's time we talk about Denmark."

My heart sped up and began to pound harder at the mention of Denmark.

"Finally?" I queried.

"Yes, finally," he replied.

We left the chapel and walked into the house and went to the library where Papa's small private soundproof office was hidden. Here, we would be able to speak freely without having to deal with the fear of being overheard.

Gabe and Ralph, who were on continued assignment guarding Christopher, joined us. We sat down together at a small conference table and slowly and carefully Chris began to give me some of the details of his mysterious trip to Denmark.

"British intelligence is consistently monitoring the travels of those individuals they consider 'suspicious' and who might pose a threat to their national security. Over the past several months they've become particularly aware of a new personality that has quietly but quickly emerged on the scene of international politics; he's a virtual unknown but for reasons no one can figure out, he appears to be developing a strong following. He's dramatic and charismatic and has made political and social connections of the highest level, some even in royal households."

"Interpol has been unable to authenticate his dossier; his passport lists Italy as his birthplace but England as his residence. And while his file appears flawless we have every reason to believe that it is nothing more than an ingenious fabrication; his name is Adriano Rinaldi," Gabe added.

"He began to appear at key events around Europe only recently; and when his name began to surface in a variety of data, British intelligence decided they needed to investigate further," Ralph said as he began to give a chronological account of what then transpired.

"Our first attempt to interview him was through regular channels; he declined our invitation and having no authority or reason to pursue him, we backed away. We then asked an undercover operative, working for a worldwide news magazine, to interview him, but he refused that as well. It's impossible to get close enough to talk to him even casually because he's surrounded by security wherever he goes," Gabe continued.

"Why?" I asked, confused.

"Good question," Gabe answered. "Why would a virtual 'nobody' need security?"

"Perhaps he's really a 'somebody' having a little fun traveling incognito," I offered.

"If that's so, why hide from the authorities?" Ralph asked.

"Just to be difficult, perhaps," I added. "Do you have a picture of him that I might see?" I then asked.

"No, at least not one that's very good. He doesn't like to have his picture taken, or so we've been told, due to his deformities."

"Deformities?" I asked, "What kind?"

"He has a large scar over his eye; the story he tells is that he was burned in a fire; he's having ongoing cosmetic surgery and skin grafting on his face, hands and arms. His passport lists his age as forty but he looks older; probably because his hair is completely white," Ralph continued.

"A team of two agents were dispatched to keep him under surveillance while he was in Rome a few months ago; they were both murdered. A second team was sent to replace them in Paris when he surfaced there and they met the same fate."

"I was contacted," Chris began his narrative once again, "after the second team failed. Mr. Rinaldi and his party had traveled to Cannes to schmooze with the rich and famous; and since my celebrity status gives me access to venues that are closed to others, it seemed possible that I could do what the others could not: surveil him in the open."

"Internet chatter tipped us off that a large and important gathering was going to take place in Copenhagen; that's why we asked Chris to go to Denmark since he's familiar with many of the social elites of the country. We were sure his presence would bring in a cluster of invitations to any social events being held, and it did," Gabe said slowly.

I remained quiet while Chris and the Shomer twins continued to explain all that had transpired while they were traveling in Denmark; Chris attended a number of informal gatherings and high-powered dinner parties. He dined with the famous and occasionally with the ignominious, treating both I was sure with the same gracious behavior.

"Did you ever have an opportunity to meet with or speak to Rinaldi?" I asked Chris inquisitively.

"No, although I got very close several times; whenever I approached him his bodyguards politely cast me aside."

"Didn't that seem terribly strange?" I replied, my curiosity piqued, knowing most people wanted to meet Christopher if given the opportunity.

"It did," Chris answered. "Nevertheless, I watched him from a distance always carefully listening to the chatter going on. There were those who were eager to share what little bit of knowledge they had of him; I thought at the time that his elusiveness was part of his game to drive up his appeal."

"But you don't believe that to be true now?" I said.

"No, I do think it's true; I just don't think it's solely true. If an attempt hadn't been made on my life, I probably wouldn't be in the position to think what I think now," Chris said pensively.

"Which is?"

"That he was purposefully hiding from me!"

"From you, Chris," I questioned. "Why?"

"That, my darling, is what we need to find out. Actually, we're not even sure the attempt on my life was orchestrated by him or his confederates; we are simply assuming there's a connection because of what happened to previous agents."

"We knew there was a certain amount of risk involved in this assignment, Rachel, but Chris as an international celebrity should never have been suspected as anything more than what he is. We took special precautions to keep him from being linked to our activities, which is why we asked him to maintain telephone silence during his stay in Europe. Gabe and I remained in the background whenever he went out in public; a team of agents working as hired security guards were his escorts. Anyone who knows him knows he has always had security with him so to forego it would seem unnatural," Ralph explained and then went on to say, "We kept his travel itinerary a secret so no one could know when or where he was scheduled to arrive in the U.S.; we boarded each flight he was on late, in the event anyone was watching."

"Then how is it possible that an assassin was waiting for Chris at the airport?" I asked, concerned.

"Apparently the assassins were at the airport for a few days; we were able to identity the man who was killed on airport security tapes. It seems they were waiting to see if Chris would be on one of the incoming flights since it's the closest airport to your home, but we just don't know," Gabe replied.

"Now, we need to deal with the issue at hand," Chris said, stating the obvious. "I have no desire to put my family or friends in danger; and until we know why someone attempted to murder me, I have to remain as remote and inaccessible to the public as possible.

"My injury is a perfect cover for the time being; this week my office is going to release an announcement to the public stating that due to medical complications I will be incapacitated for the next six to twelve months."

I looked at him perplexed. "You're not going to continue with this, are you?"

"Rachel, I must," he said decisively.

"But Christopher…,"

"Rachel," he said taking hold of my hands, "everything will be fine. I don't have a choice in the matter; I need to continue. I'll work behind the scenes as much as possible; Ralph has arranged for me to meet with a few select gentlemen and together we're going to work to find out what's going on in Europe. It must be terribly serious or this group of men would not have endeavored to eliminate me."

"Under normal circumstances, Rachel, you would not be privy to this information; however, since Christopher seems to be an unknown element in this entire situation, we felt it was absolutely necessary for you to know what has transpired and that there is an element of danger in continuing," Gabe said with a note of finality.

I felt helpless and bewildered; Chris would never turn back

now. And as much as I didn't want him to be in a place of danger, I had to support him.

"Well," I said softly, "where God leads we follow."

Chris gave me a hug and then proceeded to tell me his plans for the future.

Chapter Thirty-four

Saying Farewell

*V*ianca had flown to New York with Wesley's body while Chris was still in the hospital; she and his parents had agreed he should be buried in his hometown. When Chris was better we held a small but intimate memorial in Santa Monica to remember our faithful friend. He had been a part of our "family" for so long our hearts ached when we spoke his name. Wesley had been a good man and a very kind man; an excellent listener and an able advisor and next to James Hamilton, he had been Christopher's closest friend. His murderers would eventually be brought to justice, because I knew finding those responsible for his death was now a part of Chris's personal quest.

The weather was still warm when the school year began and even our youngest grandchildren, Ethan and Caitlin, were attending preschool classes three mornings a week. Allen returned to his college curriculum and Edgar to his high school students. Charlotte, who taught music from home, began preparing for her Christmas music recital as she now had thirty students to train.

Devon was once again engrossed in her research, and Dari was progressing rapidly in her independent studies and improving her Hebrew; she had received a few letters from her friend Leah who lived in the north of Israel. Her parents issued an open invitation to them to visit their home and country anytime and Devon hesitantly agreed to consider a trip in the spring.

Victoria had enrolled in an art class and was looking forward to exploring the depths of her abilities, while Chloe was *painfully* enduring her first real mornings of solitude while her daughter went to school for the first time.

Paul had met with our three daughters and Chloe to personally apologize for Jessica's behavior; she had filed for divorce. He had been true to his word and in the days that followed our initial meeting several retractions appeared in both the print and electronic media along with apologies regarding the allegations made against Chris and his character.

Sophie had moved home with her mother permanently and Maggie had been installed as the resident manager of the inn. So far, things were working out well; Miriam was able to help when questions arose and Sadie handled reservations. In time, Maggie would begin to learn the basics of operating a computer. And Martha, my dear friend Martha, was truly happy to have Maggie nearby.

Noah was especially busy. He was taken by surprise when Roberto Ortiz, his assistant, suddenly resigned to accept a lucrative position in Argentina; fortunately, Hector Guirmo was already preparing to take his place.

Patrick and Patricia were always busy but I sensed a newfound joy in this childless couple, which came, I believed, as a result of the work they were doing with the young people now living at the ranch.

Prudence and Sam were different; the shootout at the airport had changed them dramatically. The first nuances of their new relationship appeared shortly thereafter and were confirmed by her when she came to tell me they realized they were in love.

Woody and Zanna were perfect in Petaluma; and we were especially pleased to hear they were finally expecting their first child. Miriam and Noah and Hannah and Adam were all growing closer; it wouldn't be long before they would all be planning a wedding.

Marie and Thomas had celebrated their anniversary by taking

a restful trip to Greece, which delayed our annual summer holiday together but it was gratifying to see her healthy and happy once again.

John and Sarah Edwards were busy little bees and happier than ever serving God and the community. Julio located a temporary facility in town in which we could hold church services, and a member of the congregation was able to rent them a small home until the parsonage could be rebuilt; they were elated with both.

By September the preparations for our fall women's conference, scheduled for the first weekend of October, were complete. I was looking forward to hearing Myra speak socially for the first time and happily spent several days at the end of the month assisting the decorating committee busily preparing for the weekend.

The two-day event consisted of a worship service on Friday evening to be followed by beverages and desserts; late Saturday morning the ladies would enjoy a delectable brunch and then be treated to a heavenly spiritual meal served by our guest speaker, Myra Clayborn.

The chosen table décor was designed to reflect this year's theme: Standing upon the Rock. Brown and blue linens were selected to represent the earth and the sky. As a special surprise we ordered inspirational stones for each attendee; they came in a variety of colors and shapes and were engraved with a motivating word. I owned two that I had received from friends in previous years to memorialize special events. I kept them on my desk to use as paperweights.

The centerpieces, crafted by Paige Payton, a local artisan who also attended our church, consisted of shallow ceramic bowls made from dark brown clay filled slightly with light-colored sand topped with a sturdy piece of granite. And since Myra's message would, in part, revolve around pottery, I suggested we consider having Paige give a practical demonstration of her craft; she agreed.

Paige Payton was a tall young woman with long reddish brown hair; her delicate complexion was lightly dotted with a smattering of freckles and she had a beautiful smile. She produced both functional ceramics and lovely art objects; she even created her own line of animal figurines that she called "Paige's Pets."

Marie arrived on Thursday and when her car pulled into the

driveway in front of the house she was wearing her pretty pink hat; I was sitting on the front porch awaiting her arrival and wearing mine as well. They weren't fancy chapeaus they were simply symbols of our friendship: a token of love given at a difficult time. And even though those days were over, we wore our pretty pink symbols with pride as they still meant a great deal to both of us.

We couldn't wait to sit together and have a long talk; regardless of how often we communicated by telephone or e-mail there just wasn't enough time to share all the little things that happened every day that meant so much to long-time friends. So, after dinner we took a walk and talked, and had dessert and talked and watched a movie and talked; and then we had a hot cup of cranberry-apple tea and we talked until late into the night.

Friday morning we slept in and upon arising we ate a delicious breakfast of crisp Belgium waffles with thick maple syrup, scrambled eggs and bacon. We then dressed and drove over to the ranch to verify that the preparations for the conference were proceeding as necessary; our women's planning committee, aided by my staff, had everything under control.

Myra and her team, who would be staying at the estate for the weekend, arrived shortly before dinner and were already situated in their rooms when Martha called us for the evening meal.

The aroma of freshly grilled salmon steaks filled the room when we entered. The table was decorated in fall covers of rust and brown; there were numerous ornate bowls filled to overflowing with heavenly dishes down the center. Garlic mashed potatoes, asparagus spears and carrots, spicy fruit compote and a salad of spinach and mixed greens were all on the menu. A basket of hot buttermilk biscuits made its way around the table and just before we began to eat we said a prayer of thanksgiving to God. We sipped chilled sparkling cider from tall thin glasses and completed the meal with a delicious brew of toasted pecan coffee.

As soon as dinner was over we went to our rooms to dress for the evening conference. Myra and her team all wore lovely tailored suits with the logo of their ministry imprinted on the jackets. Marie and I favored floral prints so it came as no surprise to either of us that she had chosen a lightweight floral dress in blue and I had purchased one in green.

When we were ready, Sam drove us over to the ranch in our newly purchased silver Suburban, where we met Paige busily setting up her display. She had brought several finished pieces of art and a small work in production to give a practical demonstration of her craft, which would take place after worship.

Moira had her keyboard set up on the podium to lead worship; she played several lovely choruses while the ladies entered the town hall building where we were meeting. Elena acted as one of our greeters while Laurel, who also signed for the deaf, gave instructions to those who would be sitting in the section reserved for the deaf.

Songs permeated the room for more than an hour as the ladies joined their voices to form an almost heavenly choir. Sarah introduced Myra, who in turn introduced her team, spoke for a brief time about the purpose of worship and then led us in prayer.

While we enjoyed an assortment of delectable desserts and a beverage, Paige Payton gave us a pottery demonstration, which was fascinating; it was a simple but enriching evening.

Chapter Thirty-five

Works of Clay

*T*he following morning the ladies enjoyed a delectable brunch prior to a brief period of worship. At its conclusion Sarah Edwards stepped up the microphone and introduced, for the second time that weekend, Myra Clayborn our guest speaker. Myra, dressed in a dark brown tweed suit, greeted the ladies eagerly awaiting her presentation.

"There was a time," she began slowly, "when my life was like a black and white photograph: very monochromatic. And even though I spent years trying to analyze and figure out why I looked at life the way I did, I couldn't find a reasonable answer. Fortunately, some time before my thirtieth birthday a supernatural event occurred that cleared my vision and changed my focus and brought color into my life for the very first time. That discovery is what I want to share with you today.

"My story is the story of a wounded soul; I was deeply scarred both mentally and emotionally. And while some of you may find it easier than others to identify with what I have to say, all of you may benefit, regardless, because the world is full of hurting people who are today where I once was. The good news is that there is a cure for those who want to be healed: His Name is Jesus."

Myra took a sip of water before beginning her discourse.

"As a young child, I sustained a severe blow to my personal sense of worth. The event that caused my pain was so dramatic that it left me feeling horribly undesirable. I longed for love and tenderness but when it wasn't given by those nearest and dearest to me, I began to grow hostile and resentful. Working to find love and approval through perfection, I eventually grew hard, inflexible and then desperate.

"Love became the dream I chased, believing it would end all my heartache; it was like the beautiful but elusive butterfly, which flitted away just as I reached out to take it in my hand. Continual disappointments sent me spiraling downward into a deep, dark pit of despair. Ultimately, utter hopelessness filled my soul and carried me to the brink of insanity where I sought relief through the silent door of death. And yet even death eluded me.

"My mind, blinded by pain and longing for release, was an easy target for the enemy of my soul. He quickly stepped forward whispering deceitful promises, offering a magic cure to heal my pain; he said, 'take *just one bite* of this alluring apple and all your sadness will slip away.'

"I bought the lie and took a bite and briefly, as promised, my pain subsided; the anesthetic had done its work. Regrettably, the promised cure was just a ruse and when the anesthetic wore off and the pain returned, I saw the wound in my soul was larger than ever.

"Down, down, down a dark tunnel of torment my soul plunged until I reached the bottom of an emotional pit of hell. Tearfully I cried out for release but my enemy just laughed; he kept me tightly chained in a mental chamber of horrors.

"Days became weeks and then months passed into years before a glimmer of hope shined upon my path. A messenger appeared carrying a golden invitation written as a love letter especially to me. Desperate for deliverance I clutched it to my soul and it flew as if by magic like an arrow into my heart. Joy unspeakable took hold of my being and the doorway to freedom opened bright. There in the entrance stood a Knight in shining armor holding out his hand to take mine in his. His eyes burned like fire, he was dressed in a crimson robe and upon his head he wore a regal diadem.

"He boldly drew his sword and severed the chains that bound me, and then he wrapped his robe around my unholy rags. Crying grateful tears of joy I fled my ungodly prison with him, and climbing out of the darkness my eyes finally filled with the color of new life." Myra, tears slipping silently down her cheeks as she spoke, slowly ended her story, giving us all a little time to breathe. When she did, I realized my heart was pounding rapidly, so totally enraptured was I by her tale.

"This story," she began again, "is somewhat enigmatic but it's a true analogy of my personal journey; I have been released from the devil's clutches, and redeemed and transformed for service by the Lord," she said sincerely. "I was once a captive of the darkness, dead in sin and sorrow, and a slave of misery; but I received new life by the blood of the Lamb who cut the chains of bondage to set me free."

Myra then took some time to share some of the more personal details of her life, giving us a small glimpse of the pain she endured at the hands of other hurting people.

"Victim and victimizer suffer from the same disease," she went on to say, "a fallen human nature at war with God. The devil seeks to bind us and enslave us by degrees and only Jesus Christ has the power to set us free.

"If we surrender to the Lord, he'll heal our broken hearts and even use our suffering for something good. All the horrid details of my story you'll find buried in the graveyard along with the old life that I once lived; today, I stand before you as a brand new creation walking in the light of liberty. My relationship with Jesus has taught me to look forward, pressing on to serve him every day."

Myra paused and gave a signal to Moira who was standing near the back of the room; she turned and went to open the back doors. Two gentlemen stepped forward and wheeled in a large platform wrapped in heavy black plastic; quietly they pushed it to the center of the room. All eyes were fixed on the large object covered by the tarp and we waited expectantly to see what would happen next.

"We were blessed last evening by the fascinating demonstration Paige Payton gave in clay sculpture," Myra began. "It was an interesting revelation of how a craftsman works at design. It was she who volunteered to give this additional exhibition to impress our sensibilities with the wonder of re-creation."

Laurel and Elena walked silently to the side of the platform. When Myra gave the word they gently lifted and removed the black sheet of plastic to reveal a large mound of dark brown clay.

"Out of the miry pit God calls his own and sets them on a solid foundation," Myra began and as she spoke the clay began to move. An opening slowly appeared at the top of the mound and a bent figure began to rise from within, sending fragments of clay to the floor. A woman completely covered in moist slip, a mixture of clay and water used by potters, rose gradually from the darkness of her dungeon, hands reaching upward in thanksgiving. Her eyes slowly opened and a smile appeared on her face as tears of silent joy streamed down her face. The dark brown clay of bondage washed away in silent splendor revealing the fleshly color of new life within; it was a striking illustration.

"God calls us out of the darkness of sin and into the light of his love," Myra said, and as she did Paige Payton, our clay model, stepped out of the clay and onto a piece of marble situated on the end of the platform.

"What are we really?" Myra asked rhetorically. "We are simple works of clay," she quickly replied.

"We dwell in animated clay houses that have been molded by the Master, each with its own purpose and design. Regardless of our position we must not argue with the Master; our duty is to remain pliable in his hands waiting for his return.

"Look!" Myra said, pointing toward the doors now tightly closed. We all quickly turned at her command.

"Look," she said again, "He'll soon be coming back; the day looms with certainty ahead. He's the Alpha and the Omega, the Beginning and the End; our Knight in shining armor, he's faithful and true.

"Yes, he'll soon be coming back to take us to his kingdom; his bride must be ready when he comes. He'll clothe us in fine white linen, we will shine just like the stars; just say, 'Yes, Lord Jesus, come within.'"

The ladies stood up applauding as Myra descended the platform; her team joining her to pray with those who came forward for inner healing.

Power surged through the crowded hall; people were crying and praying and smiling and sharing; it was an awesome event we would speak of for some time.

Myra's words echoed through my mind frequently as the days of autumn were drawing to a quiet end; winter and the holidays were approaching. Christopher and I were both busy and often going in different directions but we remained committed to arriving at the same end.

Hurricanes had devastated the Gulf Coast leaving thousands homeless; earthquakes in Pakistan and floods in Guatemala had killed numerous people. The Northeast was flooded and avian flu was spreading toward Europe; people feared a pandemic. The earth continued to groan and its birth pangs were growing stronger every day but many refused to believe prophecy was being fulfilled.

"One of the morning talk shows today asked their viewers to e-mail their opinions regarding the frequent disasters happening around the globe," I said to Chris while we took our evening stroll through the orchards. "They actually asked them if they thought the disasters were a part of Bible prophecy!" We came to our favorite meeting place in a small clearing and sat down on an old log situated among the trees. I held Christopher's hands in my own and looked deeply into his eyes.

"Interesting," he replied. "Did people respond?"

"Oh, many," I said with a sigh. "There were a few who agreed that prophecy was being fulfilled and some who said that type of thinking was archaic and fanatical."

"Very typical I'm afraid. We could try to do something to change their outlook," he then replied. Chris smiled at me and I knew immediately he had something on his mind.

"What are you up to?" I asked inquisitively.

He laughed lightly and then replied, "Well, ever since I had that dreadful but perhaps portentous dream, I've been trying to figure out what it means." He began thoughtfully and then his demeanor changed radically and he became intensely sober.

"Rachel, I neglected to tell you something that I saw in my

dream." He hesitated before saying anything else. I looked at him intensely, fearing what he had chosen to conceal.

"I neglected to tell you that I recognized the face of one of the men that fell into the dark city!" I gasped slightly and then horrified I asked, "Who was it?" When he uttered the man's name, I cried.

"Is that possible?" I whispered. "It was only a dream, wasn't it, Chris?" I asked, dreading his answer. "He professes his salvation openly…I know he hasn't been in church in a while, but…he used to attend faithfully…he went to Bible study and he was heavily involved in Christian service…." I stopped to reign in my emotions. Chris squeezed my hand tightly as if to render support.

"Works aren't a guarantee of a man's salvation, Rachel," he said tenderly. "We're saved by faith, although works should be the natural result of our faith. I know it's possible to be deceived, even lured away from the things that are important in life; I know there are those who completely walk away from God, too. But only those who were never truly converted can walk away forever!

"Our friend is a good man but he allows the cares of this life to sidetrack him and draw him away from God. The prosperity that came into his life, he believes is a blessing; he doesn't realize that some things aren't from God!

"And while God does allow us to be tested, we're never tested beyond what we can endure; there are times when he blesses us with material possessions and waits to see how we will react to them before he blesses us with more; but the devil watches as well; the only difference is he's waiting to see what it will take to ensnare us.

"I remember a little skit I saw at church when I was a boy," he said thoughtfully, releasing his grip on my hand. "Skits were always well-liked because many couldn't read or write. We had a popular evangelist visiting our church during a week of revival services and every night he tried to teach our little congregation a valuable spiritual principle. And one night he put on this skit:

"There were two men on stage and both *professed* to be Christians but in reality one was a spiritual man and one was a natural man. They were going about their daily lives when a third man appeared dressed in a flowing white robe, representing God; he came up behind both men and deposited coins in the left-hand pockets of their jackets. Each man looked at his coins and rejoiced, giving glory to God. The spiritual man used his coins to bless others and in doing so he transferred his coins from his left-hand pocket to his right-hand pocket; when he did, another man dressed as an angel standing on the side of the stage, deposited a coin in a treasure chest. The natural man kept his coin to himself so it remained in his left-hand pocket.

"Eventually, a different man appeared on stage dressed in a red cape; he represented the devil and he deposited some coins in the jacket pockets of both men as well. Again, the spiritual man used his coins wisely to further the kingdom of God and in doing so he once again transferred his coins from his left-hand pocket to his right-hand pocket; and as he did the angel poured more coins in his treasure chest. The natural man used his coins to buy material things for himself so his coins remained in his left-hand pocket. Throughout their lives the two men continued to receive blessings; the one who shared his blessings grew through them to become spiritually wealthy and the other who selfishly used his blessings remained spiritually empty while becoming materially wealthy.

"At the end of their lives, when they stood on the threshold of eternity, the natural man entered penniless while the spiritual man entered rich.

"It was really a very simple little skit, one I've never forgotten. And when it came to an end, the evangelist came forward to offer an explanation to those who might have missed the implication. While he was speaking the man dressed as the devil came up behind him and dropped some golden coins in his left-hand pocket; the evangelist turned to look at the glittering gold and while his attention was diverted the devil slipped his hand into his jacket and stole his wallet full of money. The audience laughed hysterically, even though they knew it was part of the skit. The evangelist smiled and said, 'Be careful that you don't allow the devil to steal those things that are truly valuable in exchange for a few little trinkets of gold.'

"We live in perilous times, Rachel, when even the elect can be deceived. Whenever I think about those poor souls falling through the wide, open doorway into the abyss, I cringe. And what about our friend? Where are the doorkeepers of his soul? Who is watching out for him?"

I sat silently and listened to Christopher as he shared the heaviness in his heart and his plans for the future. It was an adventure being married to a man that cared so much about humanity; and I couldn't wait to see where his latest vision for the world at large would take us next.

THE END

Out of the Miry Clay
Order Form

Postal orders: M.I. Scarrott
3658 Township Avenue
Simi Valley, CA 93063

Please send *Out of the Miry Clay* to:

Name: _____

Address: _____

City: _____   State: _____

Zip: _____   Telephone: (_____) _____

Book Price: $15.00 (Check or Money Order)

Sales Tax: Please add 7.25% for books shipped to a California
address

Shipping: $4.00 for the first book and $1.00 for each additional book to
cover shipping and handling within US, Canada, and Mexico.
International orders add $1.00 for the first book and $2.00 for
each additional book.

Quantity Discounts Available – Please write for information.

or contact your local bookstore

.